Starlight Comes Home

The sixth and final book
of the Starlight Series

by

Janet Muirhead Hill

Illustrated by

Pat Lehmkuhl

Previous books in this series:

Miranda and Starlight
Starlight's Courage
Starlight, Star Bright
Starlight's Shooting Star
Starlight Shines for Miranda

(ordering information on the last page)

Praise from fans and reviewers for
Janet Muirhead Hill's six book series:

Miranda and Starlight

This is more than a mere horse story. It is a journey of courage and consequences for younger juvenile readers. My own children will read this story. — *Writers Notes Magazine on presenting the Notable Award for young adult fiction to Miranda and Starlight*

This book is not just for the younger generation, but for the young at heart of any age. I would pick it up between appointments and hated to put it down until I was finished. I enjoyed it tremendously.
— *Gerrie Chapman, realtor, Loveland, CO*

All horse lovers will relate to this joyful story of a spunky young girl's journey with the horse of her dreams. The main character, Miranda Stevens, inspires young readers as she discovers the importance of faith, friendship, and integrity. — *Western Horseman*

Starlight's Courage

A must read for any young lady who loves horses. Though it is the second book in the Starlight series, Starlight's Courage is a great read on it's own. Hill successfully tackles serious issues facing today's youth in a comfortable manner making the book not only entertaining, but also educational. — *Sterling Pearce/GWN Reviewer*

The action is non-stop in this fast paced adventure with a genuine villain. Miranda and Starlight's adventures will please any horse lover and encourage their interest in reading. — *Beverly J. Rowe, MyShelf.com*

Pre-teen girls with equine leanings will certainly enjoy this, Hill's rousing sequel to the first book in her series, a great stand-alone read, suitable too for discussion group use at the fifth grade level. In this outing, Miranda is able to care for her dream horse, a rewarding task that also carries its rightful share of responsibility. Some naughty classmates provide the darkside obstacles, and of course it's up to Miranda and Starlight — and a healthy dose of courage summoned by both — to defeat the evil doers. — *www.thebooxreview.com*

Starlight, Star Bright

I am at the part in your third book where Miranda finds a puppy. It is an interesting book. All authors make the exciting part at the end of the book, but I love your books because you make the exciting parts all over in the book, which is very good. I love your books for many other reasons too. You are a great author. — *Kailey Kpropok, age 10*

The books are both entertaining and educational, touching on topics that include being the new girl at school, bullies and cliques, racism, and what happens when one lies. There's even a movie in the making based on this series and, it should be said, even boys will enjoy this series. — *www.Bookviews.com*

Starlight's Shooting Star

I know a great series when I read one! Here is one just waiting for young readers to discover! So much happens in this book. Grandpa has an accident, Miranda and a few classmates become lost, and a surprising new character throws everyone for a loop! Book four, in my opinion, is the best one yet. — *Detra Fitch, HUNTRESS REVIEWS*

Starlight Shines for Miranda

This book continues the mishaps and adventures of Miranda and her friends. Just as Miranda feels her dreams are coming true, a surprise announcement by Mr. Taylor threatens to ruin everything. Fast-paced and engaging, this installment promises to thrill readers of all ages and the growing following of this delightful series.
— *Gaydeana Eastman Hickman, Winfield (Kansas) Daily Courier*

After finishing the fifth book, I finally decided who Miranda Stevens reminds me of . . . She is definitely the modern day version of Tom Sawyer!! Her impulsiveness, ability to learn from her mistakes, and her good heart make her an endearing character, and her adventurous spirit, willingness to speak her mind and act on injustice are traits to admire. The plots of the Miranda and Starlight books are exciting and keep readers both young and old totally engaged. I will recommend

the books to all of my teacher friends for classroom reading. These are sure to get reluctant young readers going as well!
— *Susan Stanaway, teacher*

The fifth title in Janet Hill's outstanding series featuring a young girl and her beloved horse finds that 12-year-old Miranda and her black stallion, Starlight, experience a forced separation causing both the girl and her horse to go "off their feed" as their health deteriorates. The plans of Mr. Taylor (the crotchety owner of Shady Hills Horse Ranch) are in jeopardy until Starlight and Miranda are reunited and find a way to save Mr. Taylor from financial ruin. *Starlight Shines For Miranda* continues to document Janet Muirhead Hill as one of the truly skilled storytellers writing for young readers today.
— *Midwest Book Review, Children's Bookwatch*

Starlight Comes Home

This is the best book in the series!!! It deals with real problems we kids face. The ending is surprising and very good. This book tells that no matter how bad things get, you can always get through them.
— *D'Jean age 12, Montana*

This is an excellent ending to the series. Throughout the books, Miranda has grown up and matured, making complicated decisions as she went. She shows that no matter how bad things become, one must do the right thing and hope for the best. Eventually, events will come together. In my opinion, this series will attract more than just the girls who love horses. Miranda is a great role model. She is so realistic that kids cannot help but relate to Miranda and her problems. At the same time, readers can follow Miranda during all her adventures. Outstanding! ***** — *Detra Fitch, HUNTRESS REVIEWS*

Starlight Comes Home is the perfect conclusion to the time line created by the author to showcase the life, loves and adventures of Miranda and Starlight. The realistic story line with believable characters and events should be eagerly read by all. — *Carolyn A. Garber, President, Carroll County (Maryland) Equestrian Council*

Starlight Comes Home

Janet Muirhead Hill

Illustrated by
Pat Lehmkuhl

 Raven Publishing, Inc.

Starlight Comes Home

by Janet Muirhead Hill

Published by:
Raven Publishing, Inc.
PO Box 2866
Norris, Montana 59745
E-mail: Info@ravenpublishing.net

Publisher's note: This novel is a work of fiction. Names, characters, places, and events are either products of the author's imagination or are used fictitiously.

Printed in the USA

ISBN: 0-9714161-6-8
Library of Congress Control Number: 2004096197

Acknowledgments

This book, like all the previous Miranda and Starlight stories, would not be successful without the thoughtful insight and suggestions of my editor, mentor, and friend, Florence Ore.

Many thanks to Susan Stanaway and Celeste Maisel for your good advice. And thanks to the many others; Joan Bochmann, Sharon Beall, Denise Sarrazin, Zelpha Boyd, Jan and Frieda Zimmerman, and Tayla Andrews (If I left anyone out, forgive me) who proofread the manuscript.

Thanks also to Doctor Eileen White for consultation concerning veterinary medicine.

Dedication

To all of the young readers who have
offered encouragement and praise. You have
enriched my life with your thoughtful
and enthusiastic response.

And to my youngest granddaughters,
Alyssa Marie and Cassy Joye, who share
my love for horses and for books.

Chapter One

When Miranda Stevens awoke, she rose up on one elbow and looked out the window. She smiled at the deep blue April sky. There was no wind disturbing the bare yellow branches of the willow that spread expansively in the middle of the back yard. A pair of magpies in its branches squawked and twittered. Miranda had been watching them build a nest and was amazed at the large range of vocal inflections in their nasal voices. They seemed to be trying to carry on a conversation with her.

"Good morning, friends!" Miranda called to them as she opened her window wider. "Isn't it a gorgeous day?"

One bird flew up and landed again on a branch nearer Miranda. The other one only cocked its head at her. Margot, Miranda's younger foster sister, who was already up and out of the room they shared, came back to get her shoes.

"You better get ready or you'll miss breakfast."

"I'll be dressed in a minute," Miranda answered.

Another day of school loomed and Miranda felt her stomach flip as she remembered the test Mrs. Dale had promised to give at the beginning of class that Friday morning. Miranda had fallen asleep in the middle of reading the boring chapter the night before. She hoped she wouldn't fail.

"More than a month of school left! I don't know if I can stand it. What a waste of good weather! I could be out riding instead of sitting in a stuffy schoolroom all day!" Miranda complained to Little Brother, the enormous black dog that shared the queen-sized bed with her and Margot.

When Miranda entered the kitchen, she was surprised to be greeted by her mother, who much preferred to sleep late in the mornings.

"Do you realize you'll be thirteen years old day after tomorrow?" Mom asked. "Aren't you excited? You're entering a new era!"

"No, I forgot about it," Miranda replied. "I don't think a couple of days is going to change me, Mom."

"Well, it isn't everyday that my daughter becomes a teenager, so I've planned a party. I'm getting pizza, renting a movie, and I know some great games."

"Mom, don't tell me you already invited people over!" Miranda moaned.

"Well, no, I've been so busy, I didn't get my act together until last night, but I stayed up late and made invitations for you to take to school today. We'll have the party Sunday on your birthday. That should give kids enough time to plan," Mom said, holding out a small stack of envelopes.

"But, Mom, I don't want a party! I'd rather go riding with my friends like last year. Most of the snow's melted," Miranda said, as she poured milk on a bowl of corn flakes. "Margot and Elliot could go with us. So could you, if you want to."

"No, that's all right," Mom said with a sigh as she dumped the invitations into the trash. "I thought you might be ready to do some girl things. Are you going to be a tomboy forever, Miranda?"

"I hope so." Miranda said.

"Oh, you!" Mom exclaimed. "Go ahead; ride with Christopher and Laurie on Sunday, and then invite them here for a birthday dinner. We'll ask Grandma and Grandpa too. Does that suit you?"

"Yes, Mom. Thanks," Miranda said. "I hope you don't mind very much."

Mom shrugged and sipped from a cup of steaming coffee.

"May I go to Shady Hills after school, today?" Miranda asked.

"I guess so. Your dad'll be working, so he can bring you and Margot home."

"Thanks, Mom. Sorry about the invitations," Miranda said, kissing her mother on the cheek. "Let's go, Margot. Here comes the bus."

Miranda was excited about the prospect of spending a day with her friends at Shady Hills Horse Ranch, riding her favorite horse, Starlight, or perhaps helping her friend, Christopher Bergman, work with Shooting Star, the yearling daughter of his mare, Queen, and Starlight.

Miranda passed the history test, barely, and endured the day of classes as she stared out the window and daydreamed. By mid-morning, billowy white clouds rose above the mountains into the deep blue sky. *They look like flying saucers stacked on top of each other,* she thought. *Oh, there's a unicorn!* She imagined she was on its back, thundering over the hilly clouds. By the time school let out, clouds obscured the sun.

"Elliot and I might ride Sea Foam today. Want to help?" Margot asked Miranda, as they rode Elliot's bus to Shady Hills after school.

Elliot, the orphaned grandson of ranch owner Cash Taylor, was Margot's best friend. Margot's horse, Sea Foam had been moved to Shady Hills in February.

"I don't know yet. Let's see what everyone else wants to do when we get there," Miranda said.

Miranda, Margot, and Elliot met Laurie and Christopher at the Shady Hills stables just as Mrs. Bergman stopped to drop them off.

"Let's check on Lady and Queen first thing," Laurie said.

"Beat you!" Miranda challenged, running.

"Hey, wait up," Chris called.

But Miranda had already stopped short.

"Where is she?" she asked looking into Lady's stall. She strode through the stall to the paddock, but couldn't see Laurie's buckskin mare anywhere.

"Where could she be?" Laurie asked, sounding scared. "Do you suppose someone moved her? Maybe she was having her baby and had trouble!"

"Let's find Dad and ask him," Miranda said.

"Hey, Miranda! Come look at Queen!" Chris shouted. "Do you think she's okay?"

Miranda peeked into Queen's stall. The tall sorrel mare stood in one corner, head down.

"You okay, girl?" Miranda asked.

She walked along the mare's left side, patting her gently. The mare pricked up her ears and nickered softly, looking at Miranda. Both Queen and Lady were due to foal any day now.

"I think she's fine, Chris. Just sleeping. Look at her teats, though. They have a waxy discharge. Means her foal could come any day now." Miranda said in an authoritative tone.

"I know, Miranda!" Chris snorted. "She's been like that for three days. You aren't the only one who knows anything."

"There's your dad, Miranda!" Laurie shouted.

They ran to ask him about Lady.

"What do you mean she's not in her paddock? She was there this morning when I fed. I don't know how she'd get out. Do you?"

They all walked to the far end of Lady's paddock. The gate was open; not very far, but enough for a horse to squeeze through. A drop of rain landed on Miranda's nose as she looked out into the pasture for any sign of a horse.

"I'll take the four-wheeler and help you look for

her," Dad said. "She must be in the river pasture."

"May I ride with you on the four-wheeler, Mr. Stevens?" Chris asked.

"If neither of the girls want to," Dad said, "It'll be slow walking."

"I'll ride Starlight. Maybe Laurie can borrow Sunny from Elliot," Miranda said.

Elliot agreed to loan his sorrel mare, Sunny, and the girls saddled her and Starlight in record time.

It was raining steadily when they cantered down the trail along the river. As the drops got bigger and turned to hail, Miranda was glad she was wearing a helmet. She pulled up under a tree to wait for Laurie.

"Why do you suppose she left her nice stable? I thought horses were supposed to know when the weather was going to get bad," Laurie complained.

"I hope she finds shelter until this blows over. Do you want to wait it out here or keep going?"

"Let's wait. Hailstorms don't usually last long, and the horses don't have any protection. This light jacket doesn't protect me much either!"

It quit hailing as quickly as it started. It soon quit raining, the clouds broke and scattered, and a rainbow appeared on the eastern horizon. They called to Lady as they rode through the pasture, weaving in and out of the brush. Miranda let go of the reins, put both index fingers against her tongue, and whistled loudly.

"How do you do that?" Laurie asked. "You sound like a boy at a baseball game."

"I don't know what baseball has to do with it," Miranda said. "It's good for calling horses."

Instead of a horse, the four-wheeler appeared. Dad brought it to a stop a few feet away.

"We can't see any sign of her. I'm afraid she's crossed the river, which we can't do on this."

"We can ride across," Miranda said. "I know where there's a good crossing that's not too deep."

"The river's up a little from the warm weather melting the mountain snow. Be careful!"

Miranda led the way to the river crossing and tried to coax Starlight into the rushing water. He snorted and shied but finally plunged in and kept going. By mid-stream, the water was up to his belly, then up to his chest. Miranda pulled her feet out of the stirrups and held them above the water.

"Miranda, I can't get Sunny to go in," Laurie said.

"Keep trying. She's done it before," Miranda said, turning Starlight around and riding back. When she was almost there, Sunny finally stepped into the water. Miranda turned Starlight again. He stepped into a hole and was swimming so suddenly, that Miranda was

nearly swept off his back. She gasped for breath as the cold water surged around her waist. Grabbing the saddle horn, she pulled herself back into the seat as Starlight found solid footing and bounded up out of the water onto the bank.

"Don't drift downstream," she called to Laurie. "It's deep."

"So I see," Laurie called back. "I thought you were a goner for a minute."

"We'll wait here," Dad shouted. "Come back every few minutes and let us know what you find."

After a futile search, when the girls were on their way back to report to Dad and Chris, Miranda saw a willow thicket she hadn't seen before. She guided Starlight around it, peering through the branches. A movement caught her eye and she stopped. There was something in there; maybe a deer. Starlight neighed. There was an answering whinny. Miranda swung her right leg over Starlight's rump, kicked her left foot out of the stirrup, and dropped to the ground. Dropping the reins, she crawled through the branches.

"This way, Laurie," she called.

When she could stand up straight again, Miranda was only a couple of feet from Lady. A wobbly foal was trying to stand. Still wet, it almost fell over when the mare licked its back.

"Oh, Miranda, look!" Laurie exclaimed, as she stood up beside her friend. "Did you ever see anything so cute in your life?"

The wet black baby hair glistened in the fading light. A wide white blaze adorned the fuzzy face, and its spindly legs had no white on them at all.

"Is it a girl or a boy?" Laurie asked.

"A boy, I think," Miranda said.

"Moonbeam!" Exclaimed Laurie, "It's a perfect name for him. Doesn't the blaze look like the reflection of the moon on dark water?"

"You always said you'd name your horse Moonbeam, and it's perfect!" Miranda hugged her friend.

"How're we going to get them back to the stable?" Laurie asked. "He can't cross the river."

"Let's see if we can pick him up. Maybe I can hold him across the saddle in front of me."

Laurie, grabbing the colt around the chest and rump, tried to lift. He squealed and kicked. Lady put her ears back and threatened to nip Laurie. Dropping him, Laurie stumbled backward against the willows.

"Where's Lady's halter?" Miranda asked.

"Oh, it's still tied to Sunny's saddle," Laurie said, disappearing through the willows. "Miranda! Sunny's gone!"

Miranda pushed through the branches and saw Laurie holding a broken rein.

"I tied her to a tree so she couldn't run away," Laurie said. "Now I know why they say not to tie a horse by the reins!"

"Where's Starlight? He usually stays when I ground tie him, but he must've followed Sunny. Come on. Let's find them."

Miranda had taught Starlight that when his reins were on the ground, he was to stay put. She thought he had learned it well, but she'd never tried it with other horses around. She called and whistled for him as she hurried through the tall grass.

Starlight raised his head as Miranda rounded a large cedar. She called again and he started toward her, holding his head slightly to one side, trailing the reins beside him so he wouldn't step on them.

"You shouldn't have wandered off! Where's Sunny?" Miranda said as she climbed into the saddle.

Her wet jeans made it hard to stretch her leg up to the stirrup, but Starlight stood still for her. She shivered, as the cool air seemed to turn her wet clothes to ice. She got on and rode up beside Laurie.

"Want to get on behind me?" Miranda asked.

"No!" Laurie said quickly. "He's never been ridden double before. Why don't you go tell your Dad we found Lady, and maybe you'll find Sunny on the way. I'll keep an eye on Lady and Moonbeam."

When Miranda came to the river, she was surprised to see her dad in the middle of it, water up to his waist, fighting the current.

"Dad!" she shouted. "What are you doing?"

"Miranda! Are you okay? Is Laurie hurt?"

"She's fine! We found Lady. She has a colt!"

"Wait right there!" Dad shouted before suddenly disappearing beneath the surface of the water.

"Dad!" Miranda screamed.

Her heart nearly stopped as she stared at the swirling gray surface of the water where he had gone under.

Chapter Two

Miranda could neither move nor breathe for a moment. Then she sprang into action, cueing Starlight to the river bank, as she looked frantically for her dad. After what seemed an eternity, she heard a shout and looking downstream, saw him scrambling up the bank.

"Dad, are you all right?" Miranda cried. "I thought you were dead! Why did you get all wet? Now you'll freeze!" Miranda exclaimed.

"Jupiter, that water is cold!" Dad gasped. "I was getting worried, Miranda. I told you to report back to me every few minutes!"

"I'm sorry, Dad. We were on our way, but then we found her. Lady had her foal! I forgot everything when I saw him. I'm sorry."

"When I saw Sunny without a rider, I thought you were in trouble. There should be a bridge in this pasture!"

"You saw Sunny? Where is she?"

Miranda looked in the direction Dad pointed. Sunny was grazing near the edge of an aspen grove a few yards away. Miranda easily caught her and led her back to her father

"Hey!" Chris shouted from across the river. "Should I drive back and get help?"

"Just wait there, Chris. We'll be back," Dad said.

"Hurry!" Chris said. "I'm getting cold just sitting here.

"How'll we get them home?" Miranda asked, after proudly showing Dad Starlight's new son.

"We won't tonight," Dad answered.

"But Dad, they should be in a warm stable. It's going to get cold tonight. Moonbeam'll freeze."

"Newborn foals have survived snowstorms and blizzards, and much colder weather than we'll see tonight. He might not survive crossing the river, though."

"I could carry him on Starlight."

"Maybe, but what if you dropped him in the middle of the river?"

Miranda didn't want to take that chance, but she didn't like leaving him, either.

"What about coyotes and mountain lions? Lady might not be able to protect him."

"Miranda, you think of the worst possibilities! What do you propose?"

Miranda looked at her father and realized that he was shivering violently, and his lips were turning blue. What if he died of hypothermia? Frightened, she decided the most important thing was to get him home and warm. Her own teeth were chattering.

"I guess we'll have to leave them here for now, but I'm going to leave Starlight too," Miranda said. "He'll protect Moonbeam if anything tries to hurt him."

Miranda hid Starlight's tack in a tree, taking one rein for Laurie's bridle.

"You stay close and take care of your family!" she told Starlight.

Miranda rode behind Laurie on Sunny as Dad walked to the river.

"I'll get off and Laurie can take you across, Dad. Then she can come back and get me," Miranda planned.

"Oh, no! I'll wait while you take him across!" Laurie exclaimed. "The fewer times I have to cross the river, the better I like it."

"Take Laurie across first; then come back and get me," Dad said.

When they were all safely across, Miranda said, "You better hurry to the house, Dad. Ride behind Chris, so it's not quite so cold."

"Yes, mother hen," Dad said.

Miranda and her father, each dressed in warm dry clothes and wrapped in wool blankets, huddled in front of the large fireplace in the living room while the rest of the family fanned themselves or went outside for a breath of air. Miranda had soaked in a bath, but she couldn't stand having the water very warm, for it stung her cold toes.

When Grandma heard about the cold, wet pair,

she brought a pot of chili, and she and Grandpa joined them for supper.

"I don't think I'll ever be warm again," Dad complained. "That river's colder than the Atlantic Ocean!"

"I'm so sorry, Dad. It's my fault you got wet," Miranda apologized for the umpteenth time. "I should've come back before I stopped to look at Lady and her baby. Then you wouldn't have jumped in."

"Would you quit?" her dad said, punching her playfully. "You didn't push me in. I'll be fine, once I'm warm. Then I'll look back on this and laugh."

"If you don't get sick and die first," Miranda said.

"I just hope you both don't get pneumonia!" Mom exclaimed. "Maybe you won't want an outdoor picnic Sunday, Miranda."

"Oh, Mom, I meant to tell you. I need the picnic lunch tomorrow! Chris can't come on Sunday."

"Now you tell me!" Mom said. "I was going to have it all ready for you, but it's past your bedtime now, so you'll have to get up early and help me. I don't even have a cake made yet."

Everything glistened as Miranda stepped outside on Saturday morning. The rising sun painted the western mountains a deep pink. The few clouds over the eastern hills were golden. The high mountain peaks beyond Red Mountain were a dazzling white from yesterday's storm. Miranda was energized by the crisp spring air and could hardly wait to ride Starlight through the open meadows of Shady Hills. When Dad, Miranda, and Margot arrived at the horse ranch,

Higgins, Shady Hills' aging groom and trainer, met them in the driveway.

"Good morning," Dad said. "What's up?"

"I want you to look at Shadow," Higgins said. "I tried to call Doc Talbot, but can't get him. I was just on my way to tell Cash."

Ebon's Dark Shadow was the thoroughbred mare Mr. Taylor had bought last year, hoping she would bear a colt to replace Cadillac's Last Knight. With a winning record on the track as well as homozygous genes for the pure blue-black color that made Shady Hills famous, Knight brought in a lot of money in stud fees. He was past the age Mr. Taylor had planned to retire him. Starlight had been bred to take his place, but had disappointed Mr. Taylor when it was proved that Starlight could not be guaranteed to produce black foals.

"Is she finally having her foal?" Miranda asked, knowing that Mr. Taylor had been watching Shadow closely for the past two or three weeks.

"She's trying to," Higgins said, as they ran to the barn. "The foal is so big, she's having a hard time."

Miranda peered into the box stall that was lined with clean straw and warmed with a heat lamp. Shadow was lying down, head flat on the floor. Her swollen belly quivered, and her head lifted as she groaned and strained.

"Miranda, go get Mr. Taylor, and try again to call Doc Talbot," Dad ordered.

"Come on, Margot. You can tell Elliot," Miranda said.

Mr. Taylor was slow in answering the door, but

when Miranda mentioned Shadow, he grabbed his jacket and rushed past her.

"Call the vet!" he shouted.

There was no answer at the veterinarian hospital, but the message on the answering machine gave a cell phone number. She wrote it down and tried it. No answer there either, but she left a message, then hurried back toward the barn. Margot and Elliot were running ahead of her.

"Never mind the vet," Dad said, coming out of the box stall, wiping his hands on a towel. "With a little help, she emerged big and strong. She looks like she's a month old and acts like it, too."

"A filly?" Miranda asked.

"Drat the luck!" she heard Mr. Taylor shout.

"Sorry, boss," Higgins said. "There's always a fifty-fifty chance. She's a beauty, though. Looks like a winner to me. What'll you name her?"

Miranda stared at the fuzzy-haired filly stumbling around Shadow as if she couldn't make her long legs move fast enough. She was black as tar, not a white hair visible anywhere. A thrill went through her at the sight of another new foal. She was crazy about any baby animal, but horses most of all.

"Don't know and don't care!" Mr. Taylor said, stomping out of the barn and slamming the door.

"What's wrong with him?" Margot asked.

"Grandfather's disappointed that he didn't get a stallion to take Knight's place," Elliot said.

As Miranda skipped toward Starlight's stall,

Mrs. Langley, Laurie's mother, drove into the driveway. Laurie and Christopher jumped out as soon as the car stopped.

"Have you checked on Queen yet?" Christopher asked.

"Have you figured out what we're going to do about Lady and Moonbeam?" Laurie asked.

"No and no." Miranda said. "I haven't had a chance. And I sure don't want to ask Mr. Taylor how to get Lady out of the pasture. He'd bite my head off."

"What's going on?" Laurie asked.

"Shadow had . . . ," Miranda began.

"Whaaahoo!" shouted Chris. "Hurry, you guys!"

Miranda and Laurie dashed to Queen's stall. Another black foal stood on wobbly legs, blinking at the three faces that peered at him over the lower stable door.

The three friends crowded through the door to Queen's stall. They petted Queen, scratched the foal, laughed, and cheered.

"I think it's a boy, right Miranda?" Chris asked.

"Yep," Miranda confirmed. "What shall we name him?"

"Prince," Chris said, without hesitation. "His mother's Queen so that would make him a prince."

"But that's so common." Miranda said. "We should think of something unique and special. Something about what a beauty he is. See he's going to have a star on his forehead, just like Starlight!"

"He has one white sock," Laurie added. "See on his left back foot.

"Yeah, and a little ring of white above his right

front hoof," Chris added. "He sure is black, though."

"I think the white above his hoof is called a coronet," Laurie said.

"Coronet? Doesn't that mean crown?" Chris asked. "See, there's another reason to name him Prince."

"Well, he can't be just Prince," Miranda argued. "You've got to have a longer name than that on the registration papers."

"I suppose," Chris conceded, "Prince is probably already taken. Any suggestions?"

"Well, Queen of Royal Flush is the mother and Starlight is the . . ."

"No! Sir Jet Propelled Cadillac," Chris corrected Miranda, using Starlight's registered name.

"Ugh. That's such an ugly name. That's why I call him Starlight!"

"How about Royal Prince of Stars," Laurie suggested.

Miranda and Chris looked at each other and shrugged.

"That's kind of nice," Miranda said.

"I like it," Chris agreed. "We'll call him Prince."

"Or Star Prince," Miranda said.

"Come here, little Prince," Chris said, ignoring Miranda. "You are the best looking prince that ever lived," he crooned, scratching the colt's fuzzy back.

"We still haven't figured out how we're going to get Lady and Moonbeam. I just hope they're safe. We've got to see if they made it through the night!" Laurie exclaimed.

The girls met Higgins and Dad as they came from

the barn. Miranda asked Higgins how to get across the river with a horse trailer.

"You've got to drive out to the county road, and across the river bridge. Keep going until you get to the old railroad tracks," Higgins said "There's a little lane that turns off to the right just this side of the tracks. Follow it and you'll come to a gate. You won't be able to drive through it. The ground is boggy, and brush has grown up over what used to be the road. But you can bring the horses out that way. It's kind of tight, so you'd better take the two-horse trailer. Not enough room to turn the bigger trailers around."

"I'll ride Starlight back so there'll be room in the trailer for Lady and Moonbeam," Miranda said.

As Higgins had said, the ground just inside the pasture gate was soft, and there were still patches of snow and pools of water. They had to go around bushes and step over logs. But in a short distance, the ground became firm and they could walk faster.

"I'll circle to the right. You two go that way, but stay together," Dad said.

"Starlight! Here, boy! Starlight, c'mon!" Miranda called over and over.

"I'm afraid something happened to them," Laurie said. "I knew they wouldn't be safe out here at night!"

"Look! What's that over there?" Miranda asked, pointing.

"Is it Lady?" Laurie asked excitedly, but the spot of buckskin they were looking at exploded into motion and two white tails waved at them before disappearing into a growth of aspen.

"Whitetails!" Laurie exclaimed in disgust.

"Sorry, the deer are almost the same color as Lady, so I wasn't sure."

"Where's the thicket they were in yesterday?" Laurie asked. "We're almost to the river; I can hear it, but every thing looks different coming from this direction."

"I hope we find it," Miranda replied. "I hid my saddle there yesterday, but today, all the bushes look alike."

"Look, a coyote!" Laurie shouted. "I knew there were coyotes around!"

"Starlight wouldn't let them hurt Lady or Moonbeam. Trust me, Laurie!"

"I hope you're right. But why can't we find them?"

Miranda began whistling and calling again. This time there was an answering neigh. Miranda and Laurie looked at each other and then broke into a run. Starlight was walking toward them when they entered a large clearing. Miranda met him with her hand extended. He nibbled the oat cube that lay on her open palm. She petted his neck and then haltered him.

"Okay, boy. Where's your family? You're supposed to be looking after them," Miranda scolded.

"I think I see them," Laurie cried.

Following Laurie's gaze, Miranda saw them trotting toward them. Dad was right behind them.

After getting a halter on Lady, Dad boosted each

girl onto her horse, then taking the lead ropes, headed for the pickup.

"I don't know where my saddle is, Dad," Miranda said.

"I found it. Already put it in the truck."

"But I'll need it for riding back to the ranch."

"A pack rat or a squirrel chewed off the leather cinch strap last night!"

"Oh, no! What about the bridle?"

"It seems to be all right."

"That's good. I can ride bareback," Miranda said.

They had reached the marshy area near the gate and Dad picked his way carefully. Moonbeam refused to step into the mud and ran, neighing frantically, along the edge. Lady suddenly balked and backed up, pulling Dad off balance.

"Whoa, Dad!" Miranda exclaimed. "I thought you were going to fall in the mud."

"It was close! Now my feet are soaked. This mud is deep and sticky. I almost stepped out of my boot!"

"Give me the lead ropes, Dad. I'll hold them while you cross," Miranda said from Starlight's back.

Dad swept Moonbeam up in his powerful arms and began wading through the marsh toward the gate. The colt was so surprised, he didn't struggle for a few moments; when he did, Dad just tightened his grip and kept going. With little urging, Starlight and Lady followed.

Laurie swung off Lady and took the lead rope from Miranda. She led her into the trailer where Dad had deposited Moonbeam. Miranda was turning to go when she heard a shout.

"Get back here you crazy kid!" Dad yelled.

Miranda looked back quickly and saw Moonbeam bolting from the trailer toward her and Starlight, bleating in his funny little voice. Lady, who was tied inside, was whinnying and stomping. Moonbeam paid no attention to his mother, but kept running toward Starlight until they were touching noses. Then he started back toward the trailer, neighing as he ran. When Dad reached for him, he spun and sped back to Starlight.

"He wants them both," Miranda said, laughing. "He's like us; he wants the family together."

Dad followed Moonbeam who was sticking close to Starlight, and scooped him up again.

"Open the back door of the trailer, Laurie," he called. This time the colt was locked inside before he could escape.

Miranda watched the pickup and trailer disappear from sight before she turned Starlight toward the pasture. She was excited to be riding alone across an area of the ranch she had not yet explored. She looked for familiar landmarks from yesterday, but all the clearings, willow thickets, and groves of aspen and juniper looked the same.

"Wow, this pasture is bigger than I thought. But I'm not worried, Starlight. We'll have to come to the river soon, then I'm sure I'll recognize the crossing."

Chapter Three

Joyously, Miranda trotted Starlight across small clearings and around willow thickets. Surveying the deep blue sky that domed above her, she said gleefully to her horse, "See that bald eagle up there? If I could choose any animal I could be for a day, I'd be an eagle. Watch how he glides along so high in the sky. He can see everything. Oh, look there's a tiny fawn. It's so speckled and cute — and still. See, if it doesn't move it thinks we can't see it. His mother told him that!"

She hurried on, afraid that she'd frighten it. The roar of the river reached her ears before she saw it; she didn't remember it being so loud yesterday. She pulled Starlight to a stop when the river came into view.

"Hey, doesn't the river look deeper than it was? Swifter and muddier, too. I don't see the spot where we crossed yesterday."

Heading downstream, she looked for a shallower

place to cross. The churning water soon became a frothy white as it splashed over hidden rocks. She turned to follow the river upstream, passing the place she'd crossed the day before, and deciding it was too swift and deep today. When she came to a wide, but placid pool, she decided it looked better than the faster water. She couldn't tell how deep it was, but it didn't matter. Starlight was a good strong swimmer.

She urged him toward the edge. Snorting, he whirled and dashed away from the river's edge. Miranda pulled him to a stop and turned him around.

"Starlight, what's wrong with you? Come on, now. Let's go across."

She tried again, but he shook his head and planted his feet at the water's edge. When she urged him forward, he backed up and shied away.

"Starlight. You've gotta do it. We can't stay on this side of the river all day. Let's get back before they come looking for us."

Pushing him forward with the motion of her body, the grip of her thighs, and her hands on his neck, she begged him to go into the water. At last he jumped off the bank, his head disappearing for a moment. Cold murky water doused Miranda up to her neck. She couldn't breathe for a moment. Starlight lunged forward, lifting out of the water and sinking back in again. Miranda was nearly swept off his back. Grabbing his mane with both hands as his body fell from under her, she felt the water float her upward. She managed to stay on only because of the tight grip she had on his mane. Blowing and snorting, Starlight tossed his head.

He lunged forward, and Miranda's grip started to slip. Her suspended body floated downstream away from Starlight, as she reached with one hand for a better hold on his mane. She had just grasped a handful of hair when Starlight lunged again. She pulled herself over his back as he sank once more. The water had turned into black, sour-smelling mud as Starlight floundered and paddled. His back lifted her again in a powerful leap forward, then sank. This action was repeated several times before Starlight finally scrabbled for footing on the slick bank on the other side. He fell to his knees, and then flat on his stomach, and Miranda slid off to lie on the ground beside him. Starlight bounded up to stand, shaking, on firm ground at last.

"Oh, Starlight! What was that?" Miranda sobbed, stumbling to his side. "My gosh you're covered with mud and so am I. I'm so sorry, boy!"

Trembling with fright as much as from cold, Miranda began leading Starlight toward the stables. The jeep appeared out of a grove of trees and raced toward them, Dad at the wheel with Higgins gripping the panic bar. As the jeep skidded to a stop, Dad shouted, "What in the world happened to you, Miranda? You're covered with mud and completely soaked!"

"I crossed in the wrong place," Miranda confessed shakily. "It looked so calm, and everything else was so swift and deep."

"Over there? Just around that bend near the pasture fence?" Higgins sounded incredulous.

Miranda nodded.

"Thank God you're alive!" Higgins exclaimed.

"You found the Devil's Sink. I've been telling Cash for years that we should fence that off. I should have told you about it, but it's been so long since I thought about that place, it never crossed my mind."

"What is it?" Dad asked.

"It's a mud spring in the middle of the river. More than one animal has gone in there and never come out again. It takes superior strength to get through that!"

"He didn't want to go in, but when I made him, he went in fast and swam and bucked all the way across," Miranda told them.

"And you bareback! It's a wonder you stayed on! You could have been sucked into . . . Miranda, I should never have let you come back alone. I knew it as soon as I left. That's why I started out in the jeep as soon as we got back with Lady. What kind of father am I?" He held her so tight she could hardly breathe.

"It's not your fault," Miranda began, but a lump in her throat stopped her as she realized how near she had come to losing not only Starlight, but her own life as well.

Miranda finally had her birthday "picnic" in Higgins' small house, wearing his robe and wrapped in a blanket in front of the stove. Her clothes were in the dryer. They had been washed while she showered. Besides Dad and Higgins, Laurie, Margot, Christopher, and Elliot crowded into the small living room. When it was time for the cupcakes, Chris went to Higgins' refrigerator, opened the freezer compartment, and brought out a box of ice cream bars.

"Here, Miranda. I made sure we could have ice

cream with the cake. I hope you like it."

"Thanks, Chris!" Miranda smiled as she bit into the chocolate coating.

"I want to check on Starlight before we go," Miranda said when the party was over.

She had wiped him down with a towel and given him an extra large serving of oats before she went in

the house. Now that he was nearly dry, she brushed the mud from his coat.

"We need to be going, Miranda," Dad said.

"Okay. I'm almost done," Miranda said, patting Starlight's neck. "Good night, my hero. Thanks to you, I'm really going to be a teenager tomorrow."

Miranda spent her birthday on a long quiet ride into the hill pasture; just her and Starlight. She reveled in the sights and sounds of spring. Yellow fritillaries dotted the gray-green earth where sprigs of new grass stretched toward the sun. Distant snow covered peaks glistened above dark green pines and spruce. Life was good. After yesterday's narrow escape, she deeply appreciated every moment of it. Thankful for the time to reflect, she told Starlight her secret hopes and dreams.

"Someday, Starlight, you will be all mine. We'll have our own ranch, and we will do great things together. But we'll never forget to take time to explore nature like this. Look. There's an elk. Quiet. He doesn't see us yet. Wow. What a beautiful rack of antlers!"

Miranda looked in often on Lady and Moonbeam, Queen and Star Prince, and Starlight after school the next week and a half. She checked on Shadow and her filly as well. On a Thursday afternoon, Miranda saw her dad putting a new tub of minerals in Shadow's corral. Miranda sat on the fence to watch the antics of the foal who at first ran away, kicked up her heels and then returned to nibble on Dad's shirt sleeves.

She turned when she heard the jeep approach.

"Barry, come with me to find Knight. Shadow's in estrus right now. I want to see if we can squeeze one more foal out of the old boy. I'd sure like to have a colt out of this pair."

"What's estrus?" Miranda asked.

"It means she could conceive a foal, right now. She's ripe," Mr. Taylor answered.

"She's in heat," her father added simply.

"Oh. I'll help find Knight. I'll get Starlight and ride out with you."

"No," Mr. Taylor said, "Knight may still have enough life in him to challenge another stallion. Take my old gelding, Pecos, if you want to ride."

Miranda had long admired the big blood-bay gelding that Mr. Taylor used for a saddle horse. She jumped at the chance to ride him.

"We want to go, too," called Margot as she and Elliot ran to the jeep. "Can we ride in back?"

"Sure, hop in," Mr. Taylor said. "You two can help us spot him."

It didn't take Miranda and Pecos long to catch up with the jeep.

"I'll ride along the north fence and meet you where the road comes up on the hill where the salt box is," Miranda called to her dad before galloping away.

She reached the top of the hill just ahead of the jeep, but pulled up quickly as she spied a dark form lying on the ground. She moved forward cautiously as the jeep rolled up beside her.

"Is that Knight?" Margot asked. "Is he . . .?"

Knight was lying flat on his side, head stretched

out and eyes wide open. He wasn't moving and flies buzzed around his head. A small bird flew down and landed on his face and he didn't even twitch. When the bird pecked at his eye, Miranda screamed.

"NO!" She yelled sliding off Pecos and running. "NOOOOO!"

She collapsed beside the old horse, sobbing. A hand on her shoulder only made her cry harder.

"I'm sorry Miranda, but he was an old horse. He had a good life," her dad said.

She was barely aware of Margot beside her. Miranda swallowed and wiped the tears from her face.

"Why are you so sad? He wasn't your horse," Margot said.

"I never saw a dead horse before. I can't think of anything sadder than seeing a horse die."

"I can," Margot said.

"What do you mean?"

"People dying."

"Oh," Miranda said. "Your mother, of course that's sadder. I wasn't thinking. I'm sorry, Mar."

"That's okay. You didn't do anything," Margot said. "I just don't understand why you feel so bad for Knight. He was old and you hardly knew him."

"I know. Maybe it's just because of all that happened today. It could have been Starlight. I came so close to killing him again. I love him and I don't ever mean him harm!" Miranda paused to wipe her eyes.

"I'm going out of town for a few days." Mr. Taylor's voice sounded strange to Miranda. It was so hoarse, she wasn't sure it was him at first.

"I want him buried under the big willow over there. It was his favorite place. Will you see to that, Barry?" Mr. Taylor continued, "and may Elliot stay at your house while I'm gone?"

Dad nodded, placing a hand on Mr. Taylor's shoulder. "I'll take care of everything. Don't worry."

"Looks like Higgins is doing the chores," Miranda observed when she and her friends arrived after school several days later. "I wonder what happened to Dad and Colton."

"Colton went with Grandfather," Elliot said. "Hadn't you noticed he was gone?"

"I hadn't thought about it until now, I guess," Miranda admitted.

Higgins was driving the flatbed truck full of hay and Miranda, Margot, and Elliot raced to meet him.

"Where's Dad?" Miranda asked.

"He's down with the flu or something," Higgins said. I sent him home and told him I'd finish the chores. I'm not as fast as I used to be, but I'm almost done."

"Can we help?"

"If you could get a halter on Shadow, maybe you could lead her out to the east pasture with the other mares that have foaled," Higgins said.

"Sure, I'll do that," Miranda said. "Want to help, anyone?"

Chris and Laurie followed Miranda to get a halter and then to the corral. Miranda called to the sleek black mare as she approached. Shadow started toward her but when Miranda lifted her hand to touch her neck, she spun around and dashed to the other side of the corral, her neck arched. Her feet seemed to be spring-loaded as she pranced daintily along the fence.

"Come on, pretty girl. We don't have all day to play games," Miranda called, with a laugh. "Chris and Laurie, let's get her in the corner. Come up slowly from each side and I'll take the middle."

Both Shadow and her foal watched warily as the three approached. Shadow snorted, and when all three kids were within six feet of her, she bolted, almost knocking Miranda down as she ran past.

"She's dangerous!" Laurie said. "Maybe we'd better wait for Higgins."

"If we can't catch her, he probably can't either," Miranda argued, not ready to admit defeat. "I'll get some sweet feed. I know she likes that."

Shadow came just close enough to grab a bite of grain from the shallow pan Miranda held, but as soon as Miranda reached out with the halter rope, Shadow dashed away. Miranda tried coaxing her into the barn, but at the door, Shadow spilled the rest of the grain as she jerked her head back and bolted.

"Let's chase her into the barn. If we all three get behind her, maybe she'll go in," Miranda said.

Shadow ran around the corral, spinning and dashing back past them each time they got close to her. She avoided the open barn door. After several times around the corral, she finally went in. Miranda hurried in behind her to slam the stall door as soon as the mare entered. A shrill bleating neigh sounded behind Miranda as the foal tried to follow her mother. Shadow wheeled so fast Miranda didn't have time to jump out of the way. Shadow half jumped, half sidestepped around her, but she hit Miranda's shoulder, knocking her to the floor.

Slowly picking herself up, Miranda was so stunned she couldn't tell where she hurt. A moment later, she put her hand on the base of her skull and felt wetness. There was blood on her hand. She found an abrasion on her back, and her elbow felt bruised.

"Miranda, are you all right?" Laurie asked as Miranda stepped into the sunlight of the corral.

"Just a little wounded," Miranda said trying to laugh. "It's time I showed this lady who's boss!"

"Yeah, like you're bigger than she is," Chris said. "I say just leave her here until tomorrow. She'll be hungry enough then to let us get close to her."

"I doubt that," Miranda said. "Besides, I'm not about to give up now. I'll get Starlight!"

"Miranda, didn't you say she was in heat? You don't dare let Starlight get near her."

"That was last week. I don't think it lasts long. I'll bring Starlight into the corral and see if she'll follow him. If she does, you can open the gate for me, and I'll just lead them out to the pasture. If that doesn't work I'll try to drop a rope on her."

At first, Shadow paid no attention to Starlight. She was standing in a corner and her filly was nursing. Miranda rode slowly to her side with a lariat loop open and ready in her hand.

Chapter Four

"Easy boy, if I can get right up beside her, I can just drop it without scaring her," Miranda said quietly.

Starlight was more than a hand taller than Shadow. As they moved closer, it seemed like an easy task to drop the loop over her head. When she leaned to her left to do so, Shadow squealed and swung her haunches, kicking with both feet. Starlight leapt sideways and Miranda felt herself diving between them. She saw flashes of dark and light, felt a sharp pain in her left arm, and found herself lying on her back in a cloud of dust that blinded and choked her.

"Open the gate!" she heard Laurie yell. "Let them out before they trample her to death!"

Miranda looked up to see three black horses stampeding toward the gate as it swung open. Shadow was in the lead, Starlight chasing her, head down, ears laid back, nipping her whenever he got close enough.

The frightened little filly scrambled after them.

"Are you okay? Say something, Miranda! Where are you hurt?" Laurie cried.

"I'm okay. My arm hurts something awful. Other than that, I think I'll be all right."

"See, Miranda," Chris lectured. "You should have taken time to put a saddle on him."

"Maybe not," Laurie argued. "She could have gotten her foot caught in the stirrup the way she fell. Then she would have been killed for sure."

Miranda saw tears in her friend's eyes. It surprised her to see someone care so much.

"Where did the horses go?" Miranda asked.

"Who knows?" Chris said. "They weren't wasting any time. Here, let me help you up."

As the three friends trudged up the alleyway to the stables, Mom drove in to take them home. She jumped out of the car when she saw Miranda.

"What in the world happened to you?"

Higgins walked up, shaking his head before Miranda could reply.

"When I asked you to move Shadow, this wasn't what I had in mind, Miranda. Did you ask Starlight to do it for you?"

"Where did they go? Did you see them, Higgins?" Miranda asked.

"Yes. Couldn't miss them. They came stampeding past me. The gate to the meadow where Knight's buried was open and they ran in there. I closed the gate behind them."

"I'd better go get Starlight. He still has his bridle

on," Miranda said, turning, ready to run after her horse.

"Oh, no you don't! You stay right her and tell me exactly what happened," Mom demanded. "You're hurt, aren't you?"

"Nothing serious, Mom. Just landed wrong on my arm. It'll be okay."

Together the kids told Higgins and Mom all that had happened, sometimes interrupting each other to argue a point, and sometimes all talking at once.

"If that arm isn't better tomorrow, we'll take you to the clinic," Mom said, finally. "Now get in the car."

"What about Starlight?"

"He'll be fine, Miranda. Nothing out there he can get snagged on, and if he did, the bridle would come off before it did him any damage. We can check on him tomorrow," Higgins said.

Mom took Miranda to see her pediatrician in Bozeman the next day. By the time they finished the afternoon appointment which included x-rays, it was nearly supper time.

"Just a bad sprain," the doctor said, as she gave Miranda a sling and showed her how to put it on.

"I let Margot go to Shady Hills with Elliot. We'll go get her on the way home," Mom said with a weary sigh. "I'm so tired I just want to go to bed."

"What's the matter, Mom. Didn't you sleep last night?"

"I haven't slept well for a long time. I have mornings sickness all day and heartburn all night."

Miranda glanced at her mother's abdomen. No

longer flat, it roundly filled the overalls Mom wore. *I should help her more*, Miranda thought.

As they turned off the county road at the Shady Hills gate, Miranda couldn't believe her eyes. A small white horse in full harness lumbered toward them. Mom stopped the car and Miranda jumped out.

"Want to go for a ride?" Margot and Elliot called in unison.

Sea Foam, Margot's homely, crippled little horse, was hitched to a beautiful two-wheeled cart.

Elliot, seated next to Margot on the quilted leather seat, beamed with pride as he held the reins.

"Your cart's done!" Miranda exclaimed. "When did you get it back?"

Miranda had forgotten all about the cart and harness Mr. Taylor had given Elliot for Christmas. She had first seen it in Texas last winter, but not in this beautiful condition. It had belonged to Mr. Taylor when he was a little boy, and he wanted to pass it on to his grandson. Stored in a barn in Texas for more than fifty years, it needed new tires, new upholstery, and the shafts and wooden trim refurbished or replaced.

"Grandfather brought it back from Butte last night. We tried the harness on Sunny but it was too small. It fits Sea Foam perfectly!"

"I see that," Miranda said, walking around the small horse and examining the harness and cart from all angles. "How did you get her harnessed?"

"Higgins helped us. But now we know how and we can do it ourselves. Margot gets on one side and I get on the other," Elliot said proudly.

"But when did you train Sea Foam to pull it?"

"We didn't have to. Higgins tried her out this morning, and there was nothing to it. She acted like she already knew all about it. She's great!"

Sea Foam, the girls had been told, was born with a deformed hip and always walked with a limp. Her birth had been difficult and her poor old dam did not survive. Orphaned before receiving any nourishment from her mother, Sea Foam nearly died as well. Her kind owner nursed her as best she could, feeding her from a bottle. Without a good start, her growth was stunted and her head always seemed too big for her body. Yet Margot, who had never cared much about horses before, fell in love with her and had to have her for her own. She named her Sea Foam because of her color, a

dingy greenish-yellow and white.

"May I ride with them back to the stable, Mom?"

"Not this time. You don't need to take any chances of falling on your arm again. Besides, you don't have your helmet."

"But, Mom," Miranda began, but a look from her mother told her it was better not to argue.

Higgins met them in front of the stables.

"What about Starlight? Is he still out in the pasture with his bridle on?"

"No, Colton and I got him in this morning and put Shadow and her foal in with the rest of the brood mares. He lost his bridle. You can look for it the next time you go riding."

When school let out for the summer, Miranda was busy from early morning until late at night each day. There were foals to play with, horses to ride, chores to do, both at home and at Shady Hills. She often rode with Margot and Elliot in his cart. Sea Foam didn't seem to mind pulling it, though she limped a little more at the end of the day.

Higgins, Dad, Colton, and Mr. Taylor were all busy with the many details of keeping a horse ranch up and running profitably. Dad hardly had time to work on the improvements he wanted to make to the Caruthers Place, which he now owned. Mom had all she could do to take care of the house and four-year-old Kort. The morning sickness that had plagued her throughout the spring had finally stopped, but as her belly expanded, she tired more easily.

Miranda was happy to take care of the lively, curious Kort while Mom napped, but it was Margot who most often stayed home to help. Although Kort and Margot hadn't always been part of Miranda's life, she considered them her siblings. Miranda's mom had been Kort's nanny when he was a toddler, and later adopted him when his mother decided she no longer had time for him. Margot had come to live with them when her mother died, and soon became an integral part of the family.

At Shady Hills, Miranda often heard Mr. Taylor complain that there just wasn't enough money to go around. She didn't believe it, but thought he was hinting that they should race Starlight again. She would never agree! Racing only took Starlight away from her. Mr. Taylor took other horses to races across the country. Colton, who rode them to many victories with only a few close seconds and thirds, was soon considered one of the best jockeys on the circuit. Miranda suspected that he too was itching to take Starlight back on tour, but Mr. Taylor kept his word and left Starlight behind.

When Mom said it was time to go school shopping, Miranda groaned.

"I can't believe it's time for school to start already. I sure wish I didn't have to go!" Miranda complained.

"Oh, you'll have fun once you get there. You need a change of pace," Mom declared. "I swear you're getting to be more of a tomboy every day, if that's possible. It's time you showed an interest in something besides horses."

On the first day of eighth grade, Miranda waited for Laurie at the swings so they could go into school together. How Miranda had dreaded this day, which to her marked the beginning of a season of captivity. The weather was still beautiful with leaves just starting to turn golden. The nights were cool, but the days pleasantly warm—perfect for exploring new haunts in the many pastures at Shady Hills.

"Have you heard?" called a voice from behind her. Miranda turned to see Chris striding toward her. "We have two new kids in our class this year, a girl and a boy."

"Hi, Chris," Miranda said. "No, I hadn't heard. Did they just move here?"

"The girl's parents started working for Jeffers Cattle Ranch in the middle of the summer. Her name's Jody Clark. I met her when I was working at the store last weekend. And the guy . . . Oh there he is now, walking with Laurie!"

"Hi Laurie," Miranda called, jumping from her swing and going to meet her friend.

"Miranda, meet Dennis, my new neighbor. His dad is the new physician's assistant in charge of the clinic."

"Hey," Dennis said.

"Hi," Miranda answered.

Dennis was tall with unruly brown hair and sparkling blue eyes. His smile revealed perfect white teeth and the hint of a dimple in each cheek.

"You know Chris?" Laurie asked.

"Yeah, we met," Dennis said, not taking his eyes

off Miranda.

"Hey, we're going to be late, if we don't get inside," Chris said. "C'mon, Miranda."

As she followed her friends into their home classroom, a new teacher asked for each of their names.

"I'm Mr. Carson," he said. "I'm sure we'll get to know each other well before the end of the year."

Country View was one of the few Montana schools that accommodated all students, grades K - 12 in one building. Miranda was glad she would never have to transfer to a larger school, but the budget for such a small school limited the choices for classes. Mr. Carson would teach Math, Science, and Social Studies. For English Literature they'd go to Mrs. Whitman, who also taught highschool English. Mr. Orr would teach Woodworking, while Mrs. Bell taught Chorus. For that period only, Laurie and Miranda were not in the same class. Last hour, they had P.E. taught by Mrs. Ogland who was also the girls' junior high and highschool volleyball and basketball coach. She'd been teaching all of the grade school gym classes at Country View for fifteen years.

The eighth grade class now had fourteen students making it the third largest class in the school. The desks were arranged in four rows: two with four desks and two with three desks. Dennis strode quickly to one of the only two empty desks that were together. Miranda frowned. She had her eye on those two for her and Laurie. She watched Chris take a seat in the back of the room. Laurie shrugged, sat down in the front row, leaving the only empty seat in front of Dennis.

As soon as she slid into it, Dennis tapped her on the back. She looked over her shoulder.

"Hi," he said with a grin.

Miranda couldn't help smiling in return. She turned back to listen to the teacher.

"The first order of business, I'm told," said Mr. Carson, "is to elect class officers. Let's have some nominations for class president."

"I nominate Josh," said Stephanie.

"Fine," said Josh with a smile. "I nominate Stephanie."

"I nominate Bill," Laurie said, looking across the aisle at Bill Meredith.

"I nominate Miranda," said Dennis as he poked her in the back.

Miranda wheeled around to retort, but held her tongue when he winked and smiled.

"I nominate Dennis!" Miranda shouted, standing with hands on hips facing the new student.

He only laughed and smiled some more.

"I nominate Jody!" Chris said, but he was frowning at Miranda when he said it.

"I don't want to be president!" Jody exclaimed.

"Slow down, everyone," Mr. Carson said. "Let's get seconds to these nominations while I write them on the board. One at a time, now."

In the end, Bill was elected president; Laurie, vice president; Kimberly, secretary-treasurer, and Kyle, Student Council representative.

When school let out, Miranda asked Chris if he was going to Shady Hills.

"Why do you care," he snarled. "Why don't you ask Dennis?"

"What's wrong with you?" Miranda asked. "Are you going or not?"

"I have to work," Chris said, turning away and trudging toward the general store his father owned.

Miranda and Margot got on Elliot's bus to ride to Shady Hills Horse Ranch. Laurie's mother was taking her to Bozeman for last minute school supplies. Dad, who still worked part time for Mr. Taylor, picked them up at the bus stop.

"How was the first day of school?" he asked.

"I don't think I'm going to like my teacher," Margot complained. "She gave us a pile of homework already on the first day!"

"Better get it done before you ride," Dad said. "How about you, Miranda?"

"It's okay. The classes are interesting. Mrs. Bell wants me to join choir. I'd be singing with the highschool and other junior high students, but they only have four kids signed up so far. She said she heard me sing at the Christmas program one year and thinks I have a nice voice."

"That's wonderful!" Dad exclaimed. "I think so too. You'll be a great addition to the choir."

"I told her I couldn't."

"Why not?" Dad sounded disappointed.

"They have a lot of weekend concerts and festivals." Miranda said. "I'd rather spend time with the horses."

"It might be fun, I think you ought to expand

your horizons a little."

"I like my horizons just fine," Miranda replied as she jumped out of the pickup and dashed toward Starlight's stall.

Elliot and Margot were just going into Mr. Taylor's house to do homework as Miranda came out of the stall leading Starlight.

"You want to go riding with me, Dad?" Miranda asked as her father walked toward the hay barn.

"I'd love to Miranda, but I have to take a load of hay to the brood mares."

"Dad, did you know that Sea Foam is in Sunny's paddock?"

"Again?" Dad asked. "Well, she pretty much goes wherever she pleases."

"How does she get in there?"

"Who knows? I think she crawls under the fence somehow. She hates being alone."

"How could a horse that big crawl under a fence that low?"

Dad shrugged. "I guess we won't know until we watch the little Houdini. I found her in Lady's paddock last week."

"Dad! Come quick!" shouted Margot. "It's Mom. She's in labor!"

Dad ran to the tack room and took the phone Margot held out to him. Miranda followed, leading Starlight.

"I'll be right there!" he said.

"Wait for me, Dad!" Miranda said.

She put Starlight back in his paddock and

jumped into the pickup beside Margot. Neither of them wanted to miss the long awaited event. Mom was at least two weeks overdue and complained daily about being uncomfortable and worn out.

Mom had said that very morning, "I hope this isn't a sign of how stubborn he or she is going to be. I'm exhausted from carrying this kid around! I'll be glad to give someone else a turn!"

Miranda had never seen Dad drive so fast. Grandma met them in front of the school with Mom sitting in the front seat looking flushed. Dad parked his pickup there and jumped into the driver's seat of their car, as Grandma, Miranda and Margot got into the back seat. As they fastened their seat belts, Dad pulled onto the highway and headed for Bozeman.

"Are you okay, Carey?" Grandma asked.

"Another one is starting," Mom answered, then with a groan added. "They're getting harder!"

"Over?" asked Grandma, looking at her watch.

"Just about I think, ohhh, okay. Wheww!" Mom said, "I forgot how much this hurts."

"That one lasted almost two minutes," Grandma said.

"I hope we get there soon enough."

"Why didn't you call me sooner?" Dad asked as sweat beaded on his brow. "Oh, no! What's this?"

Miranda looked ahead. A man in a bright orange vest with a stop sign in one hand was frantically waving an orange flag with the other.

"Hang on!" Dad yelled.

The car skidded to a stop next to the flagger.

"I have a woman in hard labor!" Dad exclaimed. "What's the hold up?"

"Oh, sorry!" the man said, stooping to peer across at Mom. "I can't let you through. The road's completely blocked. A semi jackknifed between the guardrails. There's no way around it."

Chapter Five

"How soon will they have it cleared?" Dad asked the flagger.

"The wrecker isn't even there yet. It just happened. We're having a roadblock put up at the junction, but I guess they didn't get it up before you got through."

"Mom, are you okay?" Miranda asked in alarm.

Her mother's face was white and twisted into a painful grimace.

Dad turned the car around and sped down the highway in the direction they had come.

"We'll have to go to Bozeman the long way," he said. "Hang on, Carey."

"They started so fast," Grandma explained as she reached up to hold her daughter's hand. We called as soon as we were sure it was really labor."

"I was in labor twelve hours with Miranda,"

Mom said as soon as the contraction subsided. "I thought we'd have plenty of time."

"Watch out, Dad, a deer!" Miranda exclaimed.

"I see it!" he said, laying on the horn and tapping on the brake.

"Slow down, son," Grandma said. "It won't help to get in a wreck and kill us all."

"Mom!" Carey shouted. "This one's harder. I feel like pushing. I can't help it!"

"Pull off the road as soon as you can, Barry," Grandma told her son-in-law.

He found a barely visible driveway to a field and pulled off the road.

"Get out of the car, girls. Barry, help me get Carey into the back seat!"

Miranda did as she was told. She held Margot's hand as they both watched the grownups.

"Not yet," Carey said, as her husband pulled the car door open and unbuckled the seat belt.

"Breathe through it. Don't push," Dad said.

Miranda was alarmed at how red and twisted Mom's face was as she panted.

"Okay," Mom finally said in a weak voice.

"I'm so sorry," Dad said as he picked Mom up and held her close.

As he moved her to the back seat, lying her down on her back, Miranda saw that Mom's clothes were wet.

"Did Mom pee her pants?" Margot whispered to Miranda.

"Of course not!" Miranda said.

"Her water broke," Grandma explained. "The

sack with the fluid that protects the baby in the womb usually breaks a while before the baby comes."

"Mom!" Barry shouted. "Another one, and I see the top of a head!"

"Stand back. Go to the other side and hold her hand," Grandma commanded. "Miranda hand me the little blanket out of the diaper bag."

"Oohhh," Mom moaned.

"It's coming. One more push and it's here," Grandma said.

Miranda squeezed in beside Grandma and tried to see what was going on.

"Give me room," Grandma said.

Miranda backed up and saw Margot kneeling on the front seat looking over the back. Miranda joined her, but all she could see was Mom's bare knee.

"Here it is!" Grandma said, lifting a wet gray thing into Miranda's view. She watched Grandma place the bundle in Mom's arms.

"It's a boy," Grandma said as the baby gurgled and then let out a lusty cry.

When they got to the hospital, Grandma took one look at Mom and yelled.

"Get a doctor quick! Something isn't right!"

There was a bustle of activity when a stretcher was wheeled out to where their car was parked by the ambulance entrance. Mom's very pale face and limp body terrified Miranda, as they carried Mom away. Not allowed to see her, Miranda's worry about mom over-shadowed the joy of a new baby.

Not until Dad called her into the nursery, and gently placed her new baby brother in her arms, did Miranda forget her mother for a few moments. Healthy and adorable, Kaden Randolph Stevens, won her heart in an instant. He weighed a hefty nine pounds and four ounces. His chubby fist gripped Miranda's little finger strongly, and she wished she could hold him forever, but Margot was impatiently waiting her turn.

Miranda felt better when she was finally allowed

into Mom's room. Mom had IV tubing in her arm and looked awfully pale, but she greeted Miranda with a happy smile. She assured the girls that she was feeling better.

"Just tired," she said. "I lost quite a bit of blood, but I'm doing okay now."

Miranda hated leaving the hospital without her mother and new baby brother. Mom, in spite of what she said, didn't look well. Finally, at two in the morning, Grandma led Miranda to the car. Dad carried the sleeping Margot.

"Mom's going to be fine," Dad assured Miranda. "Don't you worry. I'm spending the night by her bedside, and will call you if anything changes, but as you saw, the doctors have the bleeding stopped and she just needs rest."

The girls stayed at Grandma and Grandpa's house for the rest of the night. Grandpa was sound asleep in the big recliner in the living room when they got home, and Kort was sleeping peacefully in his arms. Grandma gently lifted the sleeping boy and carried him to the bed she made for him on the couch. She woke her sleeping husband and led him to bed, telling the girls good night, as they crawled into bed in the spare room.

In no time at all, Margot was snoring. Miranda covered her ears and was soon asleep too. It was just turning daylight when a heart-piercing scream awakened her. Miranda shot out of bed before she realized where she was. Margot continued to scream, sitting up in bed with her eyes glazed.

Miranda shook her sister.

"Margot! Wake up. It's just a dream. Wake up!"

When Grandma came running into the room, Margot had quit screaming and was looking confused.

"Another bad dream?" Grandma asked. "Are you okay now, Margot?"

Margot was pale and trembling, but she nodded. When Grandma left the room, Margot reached for Miranda's hand.

"Another dream about the boat crash?" Miranda asked.

Ever since Margot's mother died in a boating accident, Margot had suffered terrible nightmares. They seemed to be coming less frequently and she hadn't had one for quite a long time.

"No. It wasn't about Mother at all. It was about Adam."

"Your dad?" Miranda asked in surprise. "No wonder you screamed. I'd scream too if I had nightmares about him."

Margot looked as if she would cry so Miranda quickly added, "Sorry, Mar. That was a bad joke. I was just trying to make you laugh. Tell me your dream."

"I don't know where we were. It was a dark place, a house with lots of rooms. We were trapped inside, you and me, and every time we found another door, my father was there with a huge gold key. He locked the door and then laughed at us. Then he'd come toward us and we'd run until we found another door. Then I could only see his face getting bigger and bigger so I could see all his teeth and he said, 'That family doesn't want you, but I do!' Then his teeth got bigger and started glowing and all I could see was his mouth. That's when I screamed."

"Oh my gosh! Have you ever had a dream like that before?"

"No. This is the first time I've ever dreamed about him," Margot said with a sigh. "Maybe it's because I was thinking if anything happens to your Mom, your Grandma will have a new baby to take care of and you and Kort and. . . ," Margot's voice trailed off.

"What? You think we wouldn't want you? You're part of this family. Besides, nothing's going to happen to Mom!" Miranda exclaimed.

"Nobody knows that!" Margot retorted angrily. "I never meant to like it here. I didn't want to love this family. Now I do, so now when I have to leave..." Margot's voice stopped abruptly as Miranda stared, speechless. Margot looked so small and helpless as she fought for control. Miranda put her arms around her expecting Margot to cry. But she just whispered, "I wish I could get adopted like Kort. Then I would really belong."

"Oh, Margot. You do belong. You are my sister in my heart. No one wants you to leave."

"Thanks, Miranda," Margot said, leaning against her. "I just hope Dad doesn't show up by surprise again."

Miranda wondered where Adam was and why he didn't just sign adoption papers. He obviously didn't want to be a father. He had come seemingly out of nowhere several months ago on Margot's birthday, attempting, the girls believed, to take Mar away and not bring her back. Those plans thwarted, he had disappeared again, and they hadn't heard from him since.

A week later, on Friday, Dad brought Mom and Kaden home from the hospital. Miranda went straight home after school, eager to see them.

Holding little Kaden filled her with happiness. When it was Margot's turn to hold and rock him, Miranda noticed her mother looking on proudly. She had a glow about her that Miranda had never seen before. *How beautiful Mom is*, Miranda thought. *I hope I'm that pretty someday.* The thought surprised her, for she hadn't really thought much about her looks before. She went to the mirror to check it out.

"Hello, friend," she said to the image. "I haven't talked to you for so long, I bet you forgot me."

When Miranda was younger, she had developed the habit of talking to the little girl in the mirror as if she were a real person. It helped her sort out her thoughts and emotions when she was upset, lonely, or confused. Now she made faces at the image and scrutinized it carefully. She picked up a brush, let down her ponytail, and began brushing her long sandy hair. She liked how it framed her oval face.

"You have a pretty nose, and your freckles don't show up so much anymore because your face is nice and tan," Miranda told the girl in the mirror.

"Why thank you," she said for the mirror child. "You're not so bad yourself. Your eyes are nice with your long lashes. Trouble is, you never know what color they're going to be."

She leaned closer to the mirror and decided that they were more greenish-blue than gray at the moment.

"I think that means we're happy," she told the mirror.

Looking out the window of the school bus as it climbed the steep slope to the top of Homestake pass, Miranda let her imagination play. She loved the rock formations and imagined climbing to the tops of some and exploring the dark crevices and shadows of others. Remembering the day Adam had taken them over this road, she looked back at Margot who was sitting with Elliot. Laughing with Elliot's best friend, Mark, and another classmate, Margot seemed oblivious to the passing scenery. Grades four through eight were on a field trip to the historic Grant Kohrs Ranch just outside of Deer Lodge, Montana. The bus stopped for fuel at a truck stop and convenience store after turning off I-90 at Deer Lodge.

"If you need to use the restrooms, you can get out here. Otherwise stay on the bus," Mrs. Penrose, the fifth-grade teacher, told them.

Miranda, Laurie, and Margot got off. As Miranda walked into the store, Margot grabbed her hand.

"Look! Isn't that Candy?"

Miranda looked from Margot's stricken face to see Candy, Adam's girlfriend, walking toward them. It was her house to which Adam had taken them on Margot's birthday weekend. Miranda scanned the store for Adam. He was the last person she wanted to see. Margot clutched her hand with a death grip! For a moment, Miranda realized that Candy didn't recognize them, but when Miranda stepped aside, Candy stopped.

"Well, I can't believe it," she gushed. "What are you two doing in Deer Lodge?"

Miranda explained and asked. "Is Adam here?"

"Adam? Heavens no!" Candy said, laughing. "He left a couple days after you kids were here."

"Where did he go?"

"I don't have a clue, and I don't care. If he was half as decent as he is good looking, we'd still be together. I'm not surprised you haven't heard from him."

"What do you mean?"

"I tried to get him to take responsibility for his own kid! I hate deadbeat dads."

"Is that why he wanted to take Margot away on her birthday?" Miranda asked. "He was trying to kidnap her, wasn't he?"

"It's not kidnapping when it's your own kid," Candy said, frowning. "She's his responsibility. I want children of my own so I need to know if my husband will be a decent father."

"Your husband?"

"Adam and I were supposed to go to Las Vegas and tie the knot that weekend. We would've, too, if you hadn't come along, Miranda," Candy said with a sigh. "I should thank you. I've found someone else, now. He has three kids and takes them every other weekend," Candy added as she held out her left hand to show off a diamond ring.

"You can't believe that taking a child against her will is good parenting!" Miranda exclaimed.

"I'll be in the restroom," Margot said. "Hurry." Margot dashed away and Miranda caught Candy by the arm.

"Wait, Candy! You must know something about Adam. Didn't he tell you where he was going?"

"He said he was going back to Pennsylvania where he had some family," Candy paused, frowning. "His father had just passed away and he said his mother needed him. But I think he needed her, is the thing!"

At the Grant-Kohrs Ranch, the students were divided into groups of six. Miranda was assigned to a group with Stephanie, Jody, Dennis, Bill and Kyle. One of the parent chaperones was assigned to supervise them. They were given a list of questions to answer and told to take notes for a report as they visited various areas around the ranch.

"You have to work in pairs," Mrs. Dykstra, their adult leader instructed.

"I'm with Miranda!" shouted Dennis.

"I'll be Jody's partner," said Kyle.

"Hi Miranda," Laurie shouted.

Miranda looked up to see her and Christopher walking on the path toward the barn. Chris glared at her for a moment and then looked away.

"Hey Chris, Laurie," Miranda shouted running after them.

"Stay with our group!" Mrs. Dykstra shouted.

Dennis grinned and reached for Miranda's hand, but she pulled it away.

"Miranda, did you get an invitation to Tammy's birthday party?" Stephanie asked, as they walked down the path. "It's going to be a blast and I think she's inviting all the seventh and eighth graders. Maybe some of the highschool kids too."

"No, I hadn't heard about it. When is it?"

"October eighteenth. It's going to be in the loft of her barn."

"She only gave invitations to the boys and told us to bring a date," said Dennis. "Will you go with me, Miranda?"

"I don't think my parents will let me," Miranda answered.

Chapter Six

By the time school let out on Thursday, the first week in October, a blizzard had set in. Buses were delayed and students were kept after school unless parents came to pick them up.

"Let's go to the library and get on one of the computers," Miranda said to Laurie as soon as she heard the news.

"Since when have you been interested in computers?" Laurie asked.

Of all the kids in last year's computer science class, Laurie had done the best. The World Wide Web intrigued her and she could spend hours searching out information on history, foreign cultures, and a myriad of other subjects.

"I need to find something. Could you help me?" Miranda asked.

Racing up the stairs, they got to the library just in time to claim the last available computer.

"Okay. What do you want to look up?"

"Adam Barber," Miranda said.

"Adam? Why?" Laurie asked in surprise. "I thought you didn't like him."

"I've got to get him to let my parents adopt Margot. She's having nightmares about him. She's afraid he'll take her away from us."

"Maybe if you find him he will."

"That would be terrible, but I don't see why he would. He hasn't called or written to her since he was here almost a year ago."

Laurie's fingers were already flying over the keyboard. "Here's one in Allentown, Pennsylvania."

"Maybe that's him!" Miranda exclaimed, thrilled that it could be so easy. "Candy said his parents lived in Pennsylvania."

"Okay. This guy is a graphic designer and an architect with both a school and a home address. Looks like a college professor."

"Oh," Miranda said flatly. "That can't be him."

"Here's a genealogy site."

Miranda looked at the screen. It listed several Adam Barbers born in England in the sixteen hundreds. She sighed.

Laurie tried again, clicking on a link to "Adam Barber; living." But then the computer shut down as the power went off, leaving the library almost dark.

"Shoot. We'll have to try later, I guess," Miranda

said with a sigh.

"I'm afraid it's not going to be easy. We just looked at two sites so far. There are hundreds."

"Adam Barber is too common," Miranda sighed.

"Laurie, I'm ready to go home now," said Mr. Langley, Laurie's dad and the sixth grade teacher. "Miranda and Margot are welcome to come over and stay with us until the storm clears. I called the Stevens and they said it would be fine."

The snow was coming down hard and fast, making it hard to see, but stores and buildings blocked most of the wind. After walking the few blocks to the Langleys' house, they all looked like white icing had been dumped on them. Mrs. Langley greeted them on the front veranda with a broom.

"Here, let me brush the snow off before you bring it in to melt on my floor," she said, laughing.

Around the kitchen table where numerous candles radiated a friendly glow, they chatted and sipped cocoa Mrs. Langley had heated in the fireplace. Soon the subject turned to Tammy's birthday party.

"May I go?" Laurie asked. "It's going to be in their hay loft, and Kimberly told me Tammy's mother even hired a live band."

"Are you going, Miranda?" Mrs. Langley asked.

"I don't think so. Dennis asked me, but I don't know him very well."

"You mean this is a dating scene?" Mr. Langley asked. "I don't like the sound of that."

"It's not like a real date," Laurie said. "Tammy had the bright idea to just ask the boys and tell them they have to ask a girl. She made it a rule that the girl has to be from our school so we'd all get invited. But it wouldn't really be dating."

"Who invited you?"

"Bill."

"Sounds like a date to me," Mrs. Langley said. "I think we've made it clear that you would not be dating until you turn fifteen."

"But Mom, this isn't a date. Besides all the other girls are already going out."

"I'm sure there'll be plenty of grownups there," Miranda said hoping to make up for mentioning dating. To change the subject she added, "Remember my thirteenth birthday, Laurie? I bet I had a whole lot more fun than Tammy will."

"I think this is her fourteenth birthday. But yeah, you and Starlight almost drowned; how fun," Laurie said with a laugh. "Moonbeam, Prince, and Shadow's foal were all born about that time. You can't top that!"

"Now they're almost six months old and Mr. Taylor still hasn't named Shadow's filly. It will cost more if he waits any longer."

"I thought he had. You've been calling her Ebony." Laurie said.

"If she were mine, I'd name her Knight's Ebony Shadow. That's why I call her Ebony. Maybe I should suggest it."

"I think he's going to sell her," Margot said.

"Why? Higgins says she's going to be a great race horse."

Margot shrugged. "That's what Elliot says."

At 6:15 the electricity came back on and Mrs. Langley started preparing the evening meal. The phone rang and Mr. Langley answered it.

"The buses aren't going to run tonight. The roads are drifted closed. They'll let us know when the plows have them open," Mr. Langley announced. "If you would like to spend the night and your parents don't mind, I think it would be a good idea."

Miranda called home, got her mother's permission and learned that Dad was still at Shady Hills.

Miranda dialed Mr. Taylor's number.

"Hi, Mr. Taylor. Is everything okay?"

Mr. Taylor assured her that all was well, thanks to her dad. "He made sure all the horses were sheltered before the blizzard hit. He's staying over at the bunkhouse with Higgins and Colton. He made them a fire in the old stove when the electricity went off. He says he wants to keep an eye on it since the stovepipe is getting rusty and cracked. I've got to get it replaced before we have another storm."

Miranda lay awake for a long time thinking about the horses that were so much a part of her life. She was glad Dad was there to look after them when she couldn't.

"I know you're awake," Laurie whispered. "Are you thinking about the party?"

"No, I was thinking about Starlight and the other horses."

"Oh. I should have known," Laurie said.

"Remember when Knight died?"

"Sure."

"Well, I was just thinking how sad it is when we lose something or someone we love," Miranda said with a sigh. "It makes things like parties seem unimportant."

"I know it's sad, Miranda, but we can't just stop

living because things die."

"Of course not. But we can decide what is really important so we can make the most of life."

"Wow. You are quite the philosopher tonight," Laurie said. "I agree with you, but what about the party? Are you saying you don't want to go because horses die — and we will too, someday?"

"No. I'm not even talking about the party. Do you really want to go?"

"Yes, but I want you to go too. It won't be fun without my best friend there."

"Well, okay. If Mom and Dad say I can, I will," Miranda sighed. "That is if your parents let you go."

"I think they will if you go. You can come here and we'll get ready together, and then Mom or Dad can take us and drop us off."

At breakfast the next morning, Mr. Langley yawned as he poured himself a second cup of coffee.

"Where's Mom?" Laurie asked as she sat down with a bowl of cereal and milk.

"Sleeping in," Mr. Langley said. "We had a phone call that kept us up most of the night."

"Who called?" Laurie asked.

"Your Mom's sister from San Diego."

"Aunt Jillian!" Laurie exclaimed. "What did she want?"

"Well, it seems your cousin, Rose Marie, is in some kind of trouble. She got suspended from school and is generally giving your aunt a hard time," Mr. Langley said. "Jillian seems to think that if Rose Marie were to come to Montana to live, she'd see the light and change her ways. I think Jillian's just trying . . . Well never mind what I think."

"Rose Marie's coming to live with us?" Laurie asked.

"Seems so," Mr. Langley replied. "I was hard to convince but I finally agreed to give it a try. According to your mother, the only time Rose Marie has seemed happy was when she was taking riding lessons. So maybe getting out of the city where she can be around horses again will help. She's flying into Gallatin field this weekend."

"Yippee!" Laurie yelled. "I can hardly wait to see her. You'll love her, Miranda. She's sixteen . . ."

"Seventeen," Mr. Langley interrupted. "She'll be a senior if she can make up a couple of courses she was failing. She'll have to work hard, though, and I don't think she's in the habit of taking school work seriously."

When Miranda arrived at Shady Hills the next day, Mr. Taylor was leading Shadow out of the small pasture next to the narrow rows of paddocks that extended from one side of the shed row of stables. He closed the gate before the six-month-old black filly could follow.

"What are you doing, Mr. Taylor?"

"I'm taking Ebon's Dark Shadow to a race tomorrow. It's time to wean her foal, and since she can't have Knight's foal, I might as well let people see how fast she is. If she wins, I can sell her for a good price."

"Sell her! Why? She's one of the fastest horses you have!" Miranda exclaimed. "And I heard you were thinking of selling her filly. You wouldn't do that, would you? She runs like the wind. Look at her go!"

The filly ran around the small pasture with a graceful ease that belied her speed. Mr. Taylor took out his stopwatch.

"She's fast, all right, but I can't afford to keep a bunch of yearlings around. It's getting mighty expensive to raise and train so many,"

"But she's special," Miranda said. "She's Knight's daughter."

"I know. She's a beauty, too," Mr. Taylor said. "Maybe if her mother wins some money for me, this week . . ." His voice trailed off.

"Have you named her yet?"

"What? Oh, the filly? I'm going in to fill out the papers right now," Mr. Taylor said. "I don't suppose you have any suggestions."

"Yes, I do!" Miranda said, following him to the house.

Mr. Taylor liked her idea and wrote "Knight's Ebony Shadow" on the paper, as the first choice.

"We need to give two other choices in case that one's taken," Mr. Taylor said.

"I was thinking of Shadow's Dark Knight if it was a colt, but since it's a girl, how about Shadow's Dark Lady," Miranda said, "and, let me think . . ."

"That's all right, I'll put third choice, Ebony Cadillac," Mr. Taylor said as he wrote it.

Miranda wrinkled her nose and hoped the first or second choice would be available.

"Oh, good. Here's Doctor Talbot," Mr. Taylor said as they walked back outside. "I asked him to pregnancy test the brood mares. Well, he knows what to do, so I'm going to get packed. I'm taking three horses to enter in a couple races each over the weekend."

"Hey Miranda," Chris yelled as she walked toward the stables. "Mr. Taylor said we should wean Prince and Moonbeam. Will you help us put them in the yearling pasture?"

"Sure," Miranda agreed, glad to have Chris speaking to her again.

They watched the foals running, bucking, touching noses, squealing, and running some more. It was fun to see them making friends, but not so fun to hear the mothers' frantic neighs.

"Miranda?" Chris began in a questioning tone.

"What?" Miranda looked at him suspiciously. He didn't usually speak with such hesitance.

"Are you going to Tammy's party?"

"Yeah, I guess. Laurie wants me to."

"Miranda, you make it sound like I'm twisting your arm," Laurie said.

"Oh, sorry. No offense. But I probably wouldn't be going if you weren't."

"How about going with me?" Chris asked.

"Oh!" Miranda said in surprise. "Actually I'm going with Laurie. But you could ride with us, couldn't he, Laurie?"

"I guess. But I already asked Dennis to ride with us. He's my next door neighbor you know, and he's your date," Laurie said.

"Date! That's just a formality because of Tammy's stupid rules," Miranda scoffed.

"You told Dennis you'd go with him?" Chris sounded disappointed.

"Well, he asked me," Miranda said.

"Fine," Chris said.

"Well, do you want to ride to the party with us? I'm sure there's plenty of room in Langley's car."

"No thanks. I'll go with my own date!" Chris growled and walked away.

"I can't believe it!" Miranda heard Mr. Taylor say as she walked past Shadow's stall.

She paused to listen.

"I'm ninety nine percent certain, Cash," Doc Talbot answered. "But I'll draw some blood for a more positive test."

"But I don't see how," Mr. Taylor said. "Knight died before I could breed her back."

Shadow's pregnant! Miranda realized with a jolt. Starlight was with her the day she attempted to move Shadow to the pasture with the brood mares. But it had only been overnight, and she'd thought Shadow was past the season she could be bred. What an amazing foal Shadow would have if Starlight was the sire. Starlight was the fastest horse she knew, and Shadow almost as fast.

"Well, I guess I'll let her try to carry it to term if she's that far along," She heard Mr. Taylor say. "I sure don't like it though. She had trouble giving birth to the last one. She's too valuable a racer to be used for a brood mare. I never intended to breed her back if it couldn't be to Knight."

"Who do you think the sire is?" Miranda heard Doc Talbot ask. She waited breathlessly for the answer.

"I suppose it's that black devil of Miranda's."

Miranda bristled. She knew Mr. Taylor didn't like the fact that Starlight couldn't always throw black horses, being heterozygous (carrying a recessive gene) for color. That made no difference to her. He was the most nearly perfect animal on the planet, in her eyes.

Chapter Seven

The phone rang Saturday evening just as Miranda returned from Shady Hills with her dad and Margot. For once, Miranda got to it before Margot.

"Miranda, guess what! Rose Marie is here and she's going to Tammy's party with us, but I can't wait for you to meet her! Can you come over tomorrow?" Laurie asked.

"I don't know. I was planning to go to Shady Hills again. Maybe you and Rose Marie can go, too?"

"Rose Marie doesn't want to, and I think I should stay home with her. She's so cool! She's going to do my hair. She says it's so kindergarten. Then we'll do nails and make up. Please come over! It'll be fun."

"I would, but I'm helping Dad check on the two-year-old fillies in the far pasture," Miranda said. "I was hoping you could come."

"I would, but Rose Marie says she doesn't want to ride. She's begging Mom to taking us shopping in Bozeman or Butte."

Miranda groaned inwardly. She didn't think she was going to like having Laurie's precious cousin around. Maybe Chris would ride with her and Dad.

"Well, have fun," Miranda said. "I guess I'll see you Monday."

When she called Chris, his attitude surprised her.

"I'm not going to Shady Hills," he said curtly.

"Why not?"

"Wouldn't you like to know? I might have better things to do than to ride horses all over God's creation."

"What's that supposed to mean?" Miranda was truly baffled.

"It means I don't want to go! Why don't you ask Dennis?"

"Dennis? Why? I don't even know if he rides!"

"Listen, I'll think about it, okay?" Chris said. "Call me in the morning, but not too early."

"When I go to Shady Hills, I go early!"

"Fine. I'll call you if I decide to go."

Chris didn't call. Dad and Miranda left right after breakfast. As Miranda rode Starlight across the pastures, she was glad that neither of her friends had come. It was a gloriously beautiful day, and her father was having as much fun as she was. They raced across open meadows, played hide and seek in the willow thickets and dipped into gullies, where fluorescent yellow and amber leaves clung to the aspen and cottonwoods. They rode slowly, side by side, talking. Miranda wished this day would last forever.

Just before noon, they found the fillies, who were starting to put on winter coats, but looked well-fed and beautiful. Pausing on top of a small hill, Miranda counted them twice and announced they were all there.

"We'll ride up toward those power lines," Dad said, pointing. "There's a jeep trail that comes up from the other side to a salt box. We'll see if they still have plenty of minerals."

The view from the hilltop near the saltbox was breathtaking, and Miranda suggested they eat their lunch there. Dad agreed and they took their time. Dad identified many of the birds they saw and heard. They got back to the ranch a little before three, just as Colton was leading a wiry and skittish black horse toward the racetrack.

"You're back already? I thought you were racing today," Miranda said.

"No, just Friday and Saturday. This little lady didn't do so well, so Mr. Taylor told me to give her a good workout every day for the next two weeks."

Lady in Black Satin was a three-year-old filly Colton was starting. Mr. Taylor had picked her at the last minute to take Shadow's place.

"Come with me, Miranda," Colton invited. "You can ride along and help me put Satin through her paces."

After a few laps, Colton challenged Miranda to a race. When Starlight thundered across the finish line,

Miranda caught a glimpse of two people leaning on the fence. She sat back, cued Starlight to slow down, letting Satin catch up.

"Who's that with Laurie?" Colton asked as they jogged around the track, side by side.

"Was that Laurie? I was going so fast I didn't see who it was. It might be her cousin. Was it a girl?"

"And how!" Colton exclaimed. "Tell me about this cousin and be sure to introduce me!"

"She came from California to live with Laurie's family for awhile. I haven't met her yet," Miranda said as she looked ahead to see Laurie and a tall shapely teen walking to meet them.

"Hi Miranda!" Laurie shouted. "I talked Rose Marie into coming. Rose Marie, this is my best friend, Miranda Stevens."

"Hi, Rose Marie. This is Colton Spencer, Shady Hills' top jockey!"

"Hey," Rose Marie muttered, hardly looking at either Miranda or Colton. "Now what, Laurie?"

"Let's saddle Lady and Queen and go riding in the river pasture," Laurie said. "Chris said we could borrow his horse. Will you go with us, Miranda?"

"Hold on. I never said I'd ride. I still want to go to Bozeman. I need some things."

"Rose Marie! Mom said she'd take you tomorrow." Laurie sounded exasperated.

Miranda was surprised by Rose Marie's dark beauty. She had expected her to be fair, as she was the niece of the platinum blonde Sheree Langley. Rose Marie had raven black hair and dark brown eyes. She would be stunningly beautiful if she wore a little less makeup and ditched the frown that creased her forehead and narrowed her eyes.

"Uh, I'm pretty much done for the day. I could take you into Bozeman if you like," offered Colton.

"I thought you were supposed to exercise Satin," Miranda said.

Colton shot Miranda a threatening look. "That can wait until tomorrow. I need to get some things myself, and I notice Mr. Taylor is out of ankle wrap. I'll pick some up."

Rose Marie was finally looking at Colton with interest. A smile crossed her lips, but not her eyes. Colton, who was at least a couple of inches shorter than Rose Marie, stretched to his full height.

"That would be great, Colter! You coming Laurie?"

"Colton, not Colter!" Miranda exclaimed with a frown.

"We'll have to call and ask Mom first," Laurie said. "Besides, we planned to ride and that's what I want to do."

"You just go ahead and ride with your little friend," Rose Marie said. "I'll ride into town with Colter and . . ."

"Colton!" Miranda said again.

"I'll go to town," Rose Marie said, glaring at Miranda, "and Aunt Sheree will never need to know."

"But there's not time!" Laurie exclaimed.

"If I'm late, just tell her I got a chance to go get the things I need for school. She should be glad because it'll save her a trip. You won't mind taking me home, will you, Colter?"

"I expected Rose Marie to be blonde like your mother." Miranda commented as she and Laurie rode through the river pasture.

"Aunt Jillian is really just a half sister to Mom, and she has dark red hair. I don't know if it's her natural color or not, but Rose Marie's dad is Mexican, not even a US citizen."

"I think I see why they wanted to send her away. She doesn't seem to care what your parents say, so she probably didn't mind hers either."

"Aunt Jillian broke up with Rose Marie's dad a long time ago. Uncle Manuel wanted Rose Marie to live with him, but Aunt Jillian wouldn't let her. Poor Rose Marie! She was so sad when her dad left. He always took her to riding lessons and on trail rides. She never got to do any of that after he left."

"I wish Colton hadn't offered to take her to town. I don't think your parents'll be very happy!"

"I hope they don't find out. I hate having trouble at home."

"Humph," Miranda snorted. "I think you've got that whether you want it or not."

She urged Starlight into a gallop to clear her mind of the worry she had for her best friend. She feared that Rose Marie was bad news for everyone.

The hayloft of the Parsons' barn was clean and polished the next Friday night. The floor was smooth and shiny, and a small band was playing a fast country-western tune at one end. Miranda felt a sense of excitement, even though she hadn't been all that interested in coming. Dennis reached for her hand as they followed Laurie across the room. Miranda didn't pull it away.

"Come on, everybody!" yelled Tammy. "Grab your partner and dance with us."

Miranda watched her pull Zach onto the dance floor. Though he seemed unwilling at first, the couple was soon laughing together after Zach stepped on Tammy's toe.

"Want to dance?" asked Dennis with a smile that displayed his dimples.

Miranda glanced at the dance floor where only Tammy and Zach were doing the cowboy jitterbug, the dance their class had learned it in P.E. last year. She shrugged and nodded, wondering if Dennis would have any idea how to dance to this music. When he began leading her through some fast dance steps that were fairly easy to follow, Miranda decided it was really quite fun, but not the same as she had learned.

"Oops sorry," she said as she bumped into him. "What is this dance called? I never learned . . . "

"It's swing. I can show you all kinds of moves. Just follow me."

By the time the song ended, Miranda was laughing. She had not expected to enjoy the party, but she

was really having fun.

"Hey, you two. You looked great out there. Can you teach us how to do that?" Laurie asked.

"Sure," Dennis said, and began showing Bill the basic steps, which weren't all that different from the cowboy jitterbug.

The band began to play "Cotton Eye Joe" and the kids grabbed partners and began the dance they'd learned for that song. Now it was Miranda's turn to teach Dennis. They both laughed as Dennis stepped forward on the wrong foot and nearly tripped Miranda. He learned quickly, though, and they kept up with the rest of the couples. The next song was a slow dance.

"Let's sit this one out," Miranda said. "I need to find some water."

"Okay," Dennis said. "Wait right here and I'll get you something."

Miranda looked around for Laurie and saw her on the dance floor, engaged in the two-step with Bill. She didn't remember seeing Chris yet, and scanned the loft. *He said he had a date. He should be here,* she thought. Everyone else from her class was there. Stephanie and Lisa were sitting side by side on a bale of straw, intent on whatever they were talking about. Joey stood nearby, glancing from them to Jody and Josh who were dancing cheek to cheek, in some kind of swaying motion that hardly involved their feet.

"Dumb!" Miranda muttered.

"What's that?" asked Dennis, handing her a can of cola. "Sorry, I couldn't find any water."

"Oh, thanks. I was just watching the kids dance. Some of them don't seem to be doing anything but standing there hugging."

"Well, can't blame 'em for that," Dennis said, eyeing her with a half smile.

"Whatever happened to Rose Marie? I haven't seen her for awhile."

"I saw her outside smoking when I went looking for the refreshments. She even offered me a drag."

"Do you smoke?" Miranda asked in alarm.

"No, not regular cigarettes, but that's not what she had."

"What did she have?"

"Wacky tobacky," Dennis said with a sly grin.

"What's that?"

"Miranda, don't be naive! You know, weed!"

"I don't know. What kind of weed?"

"Good grief. Where have you been? Pot! Marijuana. "

"Oh!" Miranda felt stupid. "That's illegal!"

"No duh," Dennis said in a mocking tone.

"Did you take a drag when she offered?"

"Sure. She said, 'come on back, there's more where that came from.' Do you want to try some?"

"No!"

Miranda was stunned and heat welled up in her body. After having so much fun, she felt as if someone had just slapped her.

"Aw, come on. It's not that big a deal. Cigarettes and alcohol are worse for your health, and they aren't illegal."

"For us they are."

"True," Dennis flashed another smile that lit his eyes. "Honestly, though. It's not really such a bad thing. It doesn't hurt you, and it makes you feel good. Pot relaxes a person, and you look like you could use a little relaxing right now. How about we mosey down there for some fresh air, and you can try one puff. If you don't like it, you don't have to take another one."

"I don't think so. Go yourself if you want. I need to talk to Laurie."

The song had just ended and Laurie and Bill were walking toward them.

"Why aren't you two dancing?" Laurie asked. "I'm having so much fun! Aren't you glad I talked you into coming?"

"You talked her into coming?" Dennis joked. "I thought it was my irresistible charm that persuaded her to break down and party a little."

"Let's get some fresh air and something to drink," suggested Bill.

Miranda walked beside Laurie after they climbed down the ladder to the lower level of the barn.

"I haven't seen any grownups around here since we started," Miranda said. "Where are Tammy's parents?"

"They left right after the band started playing. They told Rose Marie that since she's here to keep an eye on things, they'd go back to the house. We're supposed to go get them if we need anything," Laurie said.

"Fine job she's doing of keeping an eye on things! When was the last time you saw her?"

"I don't know; about twenty minutes ago, I think. I'm sure she's around," Laurie said. "By the way, do you know why Chris left?"

"He was here?"

"Yeah, he and Jody came in while you and Dennis were dancing that first dance. Everyone was staring at you, especially Chris," Laurie said. "Jody kept trying to drag him onto the dance floor and he wouldn't go, so she grabbed Josh, and they've been together ever since. That's why Stephanie's crying."

"Jeez!" Miranda exclaimed. "Why do I miss everything? I didn't notice any of that."

"I guess you only have eyes for Dennis, tonight," Laurie teased. "Usually it's Starlight."

Chapter Eight

Leaning against the barn, Miranda shivered in the cold October air. The hot tears that streamed down her cheeks cooled quickly, making her face cold as ice. She wanted to go home, hide in her room, bury herself under her covers, and never come out. But she was stuck at this stupid party, with a bunch of stupid people, and no chaperone except for a self-centered teenager bent on making everyone else as miserable as she was!

Miranda choked on a sob as pressure on her shoulder warned her that someone was near.

"I'm so sorry, Miranda," Dennis said, his speech slightly slurred. "You'd better come back in the barn, it's awfully cold out here."

"Leave me alone," Miranda said, pulling away from his touch.

"Look, I'm really sorry. I thought you'd like it,

and well, everyone has to try sometime."

"That's a bunch of bull!" Miranda shouted. "Just because you can't think for yourself or dare to be different, don't think everyone's like you."

"Fine, stay out here and freeze, if that's what you want. I apologized. Now I'm going inside where it's warm."

Dennis left and Miranda slid down the wall to hunch on the ground, knees drawn to her chest, and her face buried in her arms. Besides the lingering nausea, she couldn't escape the feeling of overwhelming guilt. Maybe she wasn't any different from her friends. When Tammy invited Rose Marie to come out of the cold, and all the kids had gathered around her in a straw-lined box stall, Miranda had followed, hand in hand with Dennis. Josh had produced a case of beer and handed out cans to everyone. Miranda was repulsed by the smell as the cans were opened, and had given hers to Dennis.

When the joint was passed around the circle, everyone took a drag. All eyes were on her when it was her turn. For one weak minute she wanted to be a part of the group. Everyone else seemed to either enjoy it or act like it was nothing. She had hesitated.

"It won't hurt you," Dennis insisted. "Doctors prescribe it as a pain killer. They wouldn't if it was bad for you. I've read that cigarettes are far more addicting and harder on your health, and people use them all the time. Laurie tried it."

"Come on, Miranda. It's cool!" shouted Kyle

"Don't be a chicken, Miranda!" Stephanie said. "I thought you weren't afraid of anything."

Miranda closed her eyes, put the joint between her lips, and sucked in deeply. The taste was sickeningly sweet, the smoke burned her throat, and her lungs felt as if they would explode. She could not quit choking. She vaguely remembered leaving the barn, but wasn't sure whether she had run as she had tried to do, or if her limbs moved in slow, exaggerated motion, as it seemed. She choked and gagged until she vomited. She

remembered that!

Her eyes would not stay open. She quit sobbing and leaned back against the barn. Visions of the glowing tip of the joint as it had been passed around filled her head, as unbidden words passed through her mind, almost visual.

"Fire, fire, smolder and burn, taking your toll of each lung in turn. Why don't you drop to the straw with your light, and make a big torch to shine in the night."

I'm going crazy, Miranda thought. *And I feel awful. I'll never be the same again.*

"How was the party?" asked Dad as Miranda rode with him to Shady Hills the next morning. "You were awfully quiet when you got home last night. Did they wear you out with all that dancing?"

Miranda tensed. Did her father suspect? She felt that anyone who looked at her could tell she was a pothead, that the effect of that one puff was written all over her, even though she had awakened feeling surprisingly normal.

"Uh, it was okay."

"Just okay? Was the band any good?"

"Yeah, they were good."

"Was Dennis a gentleman?" Dad asked, looking at her suspiciously.

"Um, yeah, he was okay," Miranda turned toward the window, away from her father's gaze.

"Miranda, if he did anything, made any unwelcome moves on you, or touched you in any way he shouldn't, you would tell me, wouldn't you?"

"Sure. He never did anything like that. He was nice to me."

"Okay, I'll have to take your word for that. I just want you to know you can talk to me or Mom about anything. We care about you, that's all."

Oh, I wish I could, Miranda thought miserably. *I'd get everyone in trouble if I did. Even Laurie.*

Miranda looked for Chris, but Queen stood alone in her stall. She hoped he would come, though she wasn't sure she could talk to him about the party. Laurie arrived just before noon.

"Mom's taking Rose Marie shopping. I told her I'd rather come here so she dropped me off," Laurie said. "Can I get a ride home with you and your Dad?"

"Sure. Want to ride in the pasture?"

"It's pretty cold. How about riding in the arena. We can practice for the Winter Fair competition."

"I don't know if I want to do anything in the horse show this year," Miranda said. "Let's go up in the hayloft and eat our lunches. Maybe it'll warm up and we can ride outdoors after that."

"Okay, but I just had breakfast about an hour ago. We can talk while you eat."

"Did your parents say anything when you got home?" Miranda asked, unwrapping her sandwich.

"Just the usual, you know; 'did you have a good time?' After we dropped you off, Dad took us right home. Mom had some hot chocolate made for us. Then we went to bed," Laurie said. "It seems like they think Rose Marie can do no wrong. She barely got scolded when she came home late from town with Colton last week. He took her to a movie and then out to eat and they didn't get back until after midnight."

"And she didn't get grounded?" Miranda was incredulous.

"Dad was going to, but Mom talked him out of it. She was afraid Rose Marie would just get mad and run away." Laurie didn't seem comfortable talking about Rose Marie and hurried on. "Anyway, did you think Dad would say something about you?"

"I wasn't feeling good. I was afraid he would notice."

"If he did, he didn't say anything."

"And you felt okay?"

"I only took the tiniest puff of the stuff and I didn't inhale any. I'm surprised you did."

"I didn't really mean too, but I didn't know what I was doing. Did you ever try it before?"

"No, and I don't intend to again, but if I do, I'll just do what I did last night. People will think I'm joining in, but I won't be."

"That doesn't sound like you. I didn't think you cared what people think; when you believe in something, you usually stand up for yourself!"

"Well, I don't know if it's really wrong. There are a lot of things that are illegal that shouldn't be. Rose Marie says it's like medicine for her. She couldn't handle the pressure of school and her mom and her boyfriend and everything else without it."

"Sounds like she has a great life!" Miranda snorted. "Well, no one will ever convince me it's not harmful. I liked my life a lot better the way it was before last night."

"I have to admit life was simpler before Rose Marie came," Laurie sighed. "I used to be able to talk to Mom and Dad about anything. Now there are things I can't tell them. Rose Marie trusts me not to rat on her. And I don't want her to get sent back home. I keep thinking maybe I can help her."

Miranda bit back an angry retort.

"Let's go ride," she said. "I need to get on Starlight and run like the wind. Why can't people be more like horses?"

When Chris didn't come to Shady Hills on Sunday, Miranda fed Queen and cleaned her stall. At school Monday morning, Chris came in late and sat in the back of the room. She kept trying to catch his eye, but he never looked her way. At noon, she stepped into lunch line behind him.

"Hey Chris, where were you this weekend?"

"What's it to you?" he asked.

"Good grief, Chris, what's wrong with you? I thought we were friends."

"So did I, once upon a time," Chris said, finally looking at her with a sad expression. "So did I."

"Chris we can still be friends. Nothing's changed."

"You've changed," Chris growled.

"What do you mean, I've changed?" Miranda asked. "I have not!"

"Yeah? Well I liked you better before you got so interested in dating and dancing and getting stoned!" Christopher hissed the words in her ear before picking up his tray and heading toward a table full of boys.

Miranda was so stunned she couldn't move! She stared at Chris with her mouth wide open until a highschool boy bumped into her.

"Are you going to eat or stand there holding up the line?" he asked.

Miranda trudged to the school bus, slumped into a seat, and closed her eyes. *I'm back where I started from when I came here*, Miranda thought, dismally. *No friends and just when I need to talk to Starlight, I can't go see him.*

"What's the matter, Miranda?" Margot's voice broke into her reverie and she opened her eyes.

"What makes you think anything's wrong?" Miranda growled. "Can't I just close my eyes and rest a minute?"

"You don't have to yell at me," Margot said. "I can tell when something's bothering you."

"Sorry. I just wanted to go ride Starlight," Miranda muttered.

Grandma had called the school to tell the girls to come home after school. She said their help was needed, but didn't say why.

When they arrived, they saw Grandma on her

way to the milk barn, carrying a bucket of hot water in each hand.

"Hello, girls!" Grandma shouted. "Would you please come to the barn to help as soon as you change your clothes, Miranda? Margot, Carey needs you in the house to help with the babies."

"What's up with the chores?" Miranda asked as she walked into the living room where Mom was pacing the floor with Kaden in her arms.

"It's up to you and Grandma to get them done. I'd help but this baby can do nothing but cry today. I think he's colicky," Mom said. "Margot, would you go check on Kort, please. He's in his room."

"Where's Grandpa?"

"He got kicked by a new heifer this morning. It twisted his back and he can hardly walk!" Mom looked like she would cry when Kaden screamed louder.

"Let me hold him a minute, Mom," Miranda said. "I'll give you just a little break before I go help Grandma."

"Just long enough for me to go to the bathroom," Mom said, passing the baby to Miranda.

Kaden quit crying as Miranda nestled him on her shoulder. She walked him around the room. When Mom came back, he was sound asleep.

"Well, what do you know? You must have some kind of magic touch, Miranda," Mom said.

"I think he liked my cold jacket," Miranda said. "He kind of buried his face right into it and left it there."

"I think he has a little fever. I'll check it when he

wakes up," Mom said. "Would you put him down in his crib? Grandma needs your help."

By the time the milking was done and the barn cleaned, calves fed, and lights turned off, the temperature had dropped to zero, and a stiff north wind was blowing.

"BRRR!" Grandma said. "Let's hurry to the house. You can warm up before you go on home."

She took Miranda's hand and they ran together, laughing.

"Oh, look, here comes Dad," Miranda said as headlights turned into the driveway. "He's coming this way. He must have seen us."

Grandpa was leaning over the stove when they all entered the kitchen.

"I have hot chocolate ready for my milking crew. You, too, Barry," Grandpa added as Dad rushed in and closed the door behind him.

"What are you doing out of bed?" Grandma scolded. "You're hurting so bad you can't stand up straight."

"Hurts just as bad in bed," Grandpa said. "I'd have fixed supper, but didn't know where to begin."

"Well, you're going to the doctor tomorrow!" Grandma exclaimed.

"You better take Kaden, too. He seems awfully sick tonight," Miranda said.

The hot chocolate was bitter, but Miranda smiled her thanks at her grandfather.

"Needs a bit more sugar, I think," Grandma said.

"How's everything at Shady Hills?" Miranda asked her dad, as she spooned more sugar into her cup.

"Mr. Taylor got home in a foul mood, so I stayed after I was finished to listen to his tale of woes."

"What was wrong?"

"Seems he had bad luck at the race track. Colton was riding Sunny Side Up and got hit in the face by another rider's crop. When he almost fell off, he pulled back on the reins. He regained his balance and got back in the race, but only came in fourth."

"That's awful. No wonder Mr. Taylor was so mad. How's Colton?'

"He has a bad bruise across his mouth and cheek. But the worst of it is, I think he's going to quit."

"Why?" Miranda asked. "It's not like Colton to give up just because he got hurt."

"Mr. Taylor yelled at him for his reaction, as if it was his fault they lost. Poor kid. I think he took it very personally, not realizing it's just the old man's reaction to losing a whole lot of money."

"A whole lot?" Grandpa asked. "How much was the entry fee?"

"It's not just that. Taylor gambles pretty heavily on his horses. Sunny Side Up has been so fast on the home track, that he was convinced it was a sure thing."

"Isn't that how he got Shady Hills in trouble before?" Grandpa asked.

"Gambling gets to be a habit. The more one loses, the more he thinks he needs to bet the next time, to make

up for it," Dad said, shaking his head. "Now he's saying the only way to save the ranch is to get Starlight
back out there and 'show the world that Shady Hills
means business!' to quote the old fool," Dad said, add-
ing quickly, "Sorry, Miranda, I didn't mean to show any
disrespect for Mr. Taylor . . . ,"

"Race Starlight? He can't be serious! He promised he wouldn't!"

Chapter Nine

The next morning, Miranda dialed Mr. Taylor's number. She was nervous about calling him at home, especially this early, but she had to talk to him before going to school. It might be too late by the time school was out. The phone rang several times.

"Come on, Miranda. The bus is here. It won't wait any longer," Margot called as she rushed out the door.

Miranda wished she hadn't waited so long, but she had been afraid of getting him out of bed. She could only imagine how grouchy he'd be if she did that. Maybe he was already gone and Starlight with him. Miranda tried again at noon and, with enormous relief, heard his voice on the phone.

"Mr. Taylor! I was afraid you were gone. Dad said you were talking about racing Starlight. Please don't take him anywhere until I get there to talk to you.

You promised not to race him without telling me first!"

"Hold on, Miranda. As usual, you're jumping to conclusions. Come talk to me after school."

Miranda hurried to Starlight's stall as soon as she arrived at Shady Hills. She fed and watered him and put fresh shavings in his stall before she went looking for Mr. Taylor.

"Come in," he called when she knocked on his door. "Sit down. I want to go back to Texas and race Starlight and some other horses. In just the three days of races at Christmas time, we can pay for our trip and have enough left over to pay off some debts."

"Christmas? I'll be out of school. May I go with you?"

"That's what I'm proposing. Starlight does better when you're with him."

"If only my parents will let me!"

Kaden's loud crying assailed Miranda's ears when she got home from Shady Hills with her father. Margot rushed to take him from Mom's arms.

"What's wrong with Kaden, Mom?" Miranda asked as she took off her coat.

"He has a tummy ache again," Mom said with a sigh as she sank wearily into a chair. "Poor thing. And Kort's been giving me fits because I've had no time to play with him."

"Sorry, Mom. I thought you were taking him to the doctor today."

"He seemed so much better this morning, and it was so cold out . . . ,"Mom's voice was drowned out by Kaden's crying.

Kort was clinging to Miranda's arm.

"How about you and me fixing some supper, Kort. Want to help me cook?"

Kort clapped his hands and followed Miranda into the kitchen. Kaden, whose sobs had subsided momentarily, screamed louder. Miranda watched Margot sit with him in the rocking chair, but Kaden wanted none of it. Margot got up and paced the floor with him again.

"We're going to have grilled cheese sandwiches and soup, Kort. You can spread butter on the bread while I slice the cheese, okay?" Miranda shouted over the noise of the screaming baby.

"Miranda, I'll trade," Margot said, as she carried Kaden into the kitchen. "He's so heavy."

"Okay. I'll take him for a minute," Miranda said. "Don't slice the cheese too thick and don't let Kort get hold of the knife."

"Duh, Miranda, I'm not dumb!"

Kaden quieted for a moment when Miranda took him and began pacing. When his crying became louder, she changed his position and walked to her bedroom. Laying him on her bed she checked his diaper. It was clean and dry.

"Your poor little tummy is all pooched out," she said. "It really hurts, doesn't it?"

She massaged it gently. He cried harder.

Miranda had no sooner picked him up than he

threw up all over her shoulder.

"Eeww! Thanks a lot, little brother. It's okay. I hope it makes you feel better, "but as soon as he got his breath, he cried harder than ever.

Mom came in and took him from her. "I called the doctor," she said. "Dad and I are taking him to the emergency room in Bozeman. I'm leaving you in charge of Margot and Kort. Call Grandma if you need any help."

After changing into dry clothes, Miranda opened a can of tomato soup and helped Margot finish the sandwiches.

"You turned the burner too high, Mar. It burns the bread before it can melt the cheese!"

"So do it yourself, if you don't like how I do things." Margot retorted.

"I am doing it. You set the table."

"Don't tell me what to do, Miranda. You're not the boss of me."

"You're in a nasty mood tonight!" Miranda exclaimed. "Here, Kort, I'll put you in your chair."

"I can do it!" Kort exclaimed pulling away from her.

Miranda cut half a grilled cheese sandwich into narrow strips and put them on the bar that divided the kitchen from the dining room as Kort climbed onto a stool. He refused to sit in his highchair anymore, loudly proclaiming, "I'm not a baby."

"Margot, supper's ready. How much soup do you want?" Miranda called.

"I don't want any!" Margot shouted from the bedroom.

"Well, come eat your burned sandwich, then. The cheese is way too thick for me."

The bedroom door slammed in answer.

"Fine," Miranda said to Kort. "We'll eat without her. Here's your soup; want crackers in it?"

"Is Margot mad?" Kort asked, wide eyed.

"She'll get over it. Let's eat."

"I'll go see," Kort said, sliding off his stool.

"Kort, come back here and eat!" Miranda ordered, but he was already running to the girls' bedroom door.

Miranda sighed and took a bite of her grilled cheese sandwich. It was dry and tasteless. She put it down and began cleaning up the kitchen.

"Door won't open," Kort said, tugging on Miranda's jeans.

"She'll come out pretty soon. How about I tell you a story while you eat," Miranda said, picking him up and putting him on his stool.

"I can do it!" he yelled.

"Do you want a story or not?"

"Ooo-kay," Kort conceded, drawing the word out in a long sigh.

"Here, eat your soup and I'll tell you. Once upon a time, in a faraway wood by a shining lake, there lived a funny little dragon in a snug little cave. He didn't live with his mommy dragon or his daddy dragon, because he told them he could do everything all by himself!" Miranda began.

"Like me!" Kort exclaimed in delight.

"Yes," Miranda said, "just like you. In fact, his name was Kort. That was short for KortyWorty the Sporty little dragon."

Miranda heard noises in the bedroom and hallway as she continued the tale she was making up for Kort. She had to stop and remind him to eat now and then. By the time she finished the story with, "and so the little do-it-himself dragon was just like little Kort, and with his mommy's and daddy's love, he lived happily ever after, doing almost everything all by himself!"

Kort was through eating, and Margot had not returned to the kitchen. *Let her sulk*, Miranda thought as she tended to Kort, cleaned up the kitchen, and then settled at the dining table to do her homework. Kort went off to find Margot. When she finished her math, Miranda went to look for them. The bedroom she shared with Margot was empty, so she looked in Kort's room. They weren't there.

"Margot, where are you?" Miranda called. "Kort? Come here."

There was no answer, but Miranda heard a rustle behind the door to the guest room. She opened it, almost pushing Kort down. Margot was sitting on the bed, petting Little Brother, the huge black dog that was the family pet. Miranda stared in amazement at the transformation of the room. The hamster cage sat in the broad windowsill. The closet stood open revealing all of Margot's dresses, jackets, and shirts. The lizard tank sat on the dresser, and the picture of Margot's mother stood on the bedside table next to the lamp.

"What are you doing? Why did you move all your things?" Miranda asked. "And how did you do it all by yourself?"

"Margot's a do-it-a-self dragon, like me!" Kort said, laughing.

"Margot. I thought you didn't like sleeping by

yourself. Why did you move?" Miranda demanded.

"I just as well get used to it!" Margot snapped.

"What do you mean? I'm not kicking you out."

"Not yet."

"What makes you think I ever would?"

"Because you don't like me. No one in this family needs me. You're too nice to tell me so, but when Adam comes to get me, you'll be glad to see me go."

"That's nonsense! What makes you think your dad's coming to get you?"

"I keep dreaming it."

"And what makes you think we'd let him take you? Why do you say we'd be glad to see you go?"

"I can't do anything right. I slice the cheese too thick. I turn the burner too high. I can't make the baby quit crying. I'm just in the way!"

"Don't be stupid! You're not in the way. I couldn't make Kaden quit crying either. He's sick. Everyone wants you here."

"Yeah, right!" Margot said. "Kort even has more fun with you."

"If you don't know better than that, you're not paying attention. I think you're just feeling sorry for yourself. Are you going to move back into my room or stay here?"

"I'm staying here. You don't want me in there, and I don't want to be there. Before long I'll be out of your house and you'll be glad!"

"Look, Margot, I'm sorry I criticized you. You're a big help around here. It would be weird without you,"

Miranda said, sitting down and putting her arm around Margot.

"Don't try to be nice to me. I know how you really feel!" Margot shouted, dodging Miranda's arms.

"Oh, good grief! Just stay here, then. You won't listen to anything I say, so believe whatever you want!" Miranda shouted, backing through the door with Kort in her arms.

Margot slammed the door as Miranda walked to Kort's room.

Miranda woke from a light doze when she heard the back door open. She got out of bed and met her parents in the hallway.

"How's Kaden?" she asked as her mother carried the sleeping baby to the nursery.

"He's better now. The doctor gave us some medicine for his colic. He thinks that my milk didn't agree with him. It must be something I ate. He's getting a cold, too, and has a fever," Mom said. "Are Kort and Margot asleep?"

"Yes. Margot moved into the spare room."

"Really?" Mom asked in surprise. "I've been telling her she was welcome to that room if she ever wanted more privacy."

"That's good," Dad said. "She must be feeling more secure."

"I don't think that's it," Miranda said, relating some of her conversation with Margot. "She's been having nightmares about her father kidnapping her. Laurie and I tried to find his address on the internet at school, but we couldn't. I figured if we could talk him into letting us adopt Margot, she wouldn't worry."

"Let me see what I can do," Dad said.

Miranda saw Chris at the far end of the hallway when she came to school the next day. She hurried to catch up with him, hoping to make him talk to her about what he had said in the lunch line.

"Hey Chris, wait up!" Miranda said.

Chris stopped and waited.

"What do you want?" he asked as she approached.

"I want to tell you I'm not a druggie! I'm not any different than I ever was when you and I were friends. Why can't we be friends again?"

"Do you seriously want to?" Chris asked.

"Of course . . . ," Miranda began.

"Hi, Miranda! I've been looking for you," called Dennis from behind her. "I thought we had a date to go over history notes in the library this morning."

"We had no such thing! I don't know what you're talking about," Miranda said angrily.

"Ah come on, Darlin'!" Dennis said. "I told you yesterday . . ."

"Chris, wait. Where are you going?" Miranda yelled, as she turned to see that Chris was halfway down the hall.

She ran after him and grabbed his arm. He shrugged it off and kept going.

"Chris!"

"Your boyfriend's coming, Miranda. You'd better not keep him waiting," Chris said, as Dennis caught up to them.

"He's not my boyfriend, Chris," Miranda protested, but Chris stepped into the boy's room, letting the door slam.

Chapter Ten

Miranda stared at the piece of paper dad handed her when she sat down for breakfast. It took a moment to register what it was.

"Adam! In Pennsylvania like I thought." Miranda exclaimed. "How did you find his address so soon?"

"I'm not sure if he's there, but it's worth a try," Dad said. "It's from his military records. That's where he lived when he joined the navy several years ago. You write a letter, and I'll add a note and send it to him. If it doesn't find him, we'll get it back."

Miranda posted the letter and waited. She didn't want to tell Margot until she got a reply, afraid it would only make Margot more jumpy and fearful. It wasn't hard to keep it from her for Margot would hardly speak to Miranda, spending most of her time in her room with the door closed. It seemed she had even withdrawn from her best friend Elliot.

Miranda jumped at the sound of the bell in the middle of her second hour class one Monday morning in late November. She looked at the teacher questioningly.

"What's going on? A fire drill?" asked Chris.

"Leave everything on your desks. March single file into the hall and line up in front of your lockers," ordered a man in uniform from the doorway.

Laurie and Miranda exchanged frightened glances.

"Now!" the young man bellowed. "Get moving and no talking!"

Miranda felt her face turn red and her heart begin to pound as her surprise turned to anger. She clamped her jaws tightly closed and rose to obey the man's commands.

"What the heck is this all about?" Miranda asked, grasping Laurie's hand as they walked toward their lockers. She recognized the man talking to a group of kids in front of the highschool students' lockers. "That's the county sheriff!"

"Quiet!" shouted the young deputy who was a stranger to her. "Didn't I tell you not to talk?"

"I'm so scared," Laurie whispered when the man moved away. "Please don't do anything to make them mad."

"They have no right to treat us like criminals!"

Miranda whispered back. "We haven't done anything wrong."

"Shhh. He's coming back."

Miranda looked down the hallway to see the same deputy striding toward them with a dog on a leash. The big German shepherd sniffed Christopher, then moved on disinterestedly.

"Empty your pockets," The man demanded.

Chris frowned and took some paper, some change, and a pocketknife out of his jeans pocket.

"What are you doing with a knife at school?"

"My knife's always in my pocket," Chris retorted.

"Give it here!" the man ordered. "Those papers too. Now step aside while we search your locker."

"That's my personal stuff! You can't just go through it."

"Oh, can't I?" the man said with a mirthless laugh. "Watch this."

He started taking things out of Chris's locker, one at a time, rifling through all the books and papers and dropping them on the floor. He picked up a box of sugar coated donuts off the floor of the locker.

"I'll take these to analyze. Now pick it up!" the man demanded, moving on.

"I'm scared," whispered Laurie.

"I'm furious!" Miranda whispered back. "He embarrassed Chris in front of everyone for no reason!"

"I'm worried about Rose Marie."

Miranda stared at Laurie as comprehension

slowly dawned.

"That's it! I bet she's the cause of this raid." Miranda exclaimed. "I hope she gets caught!"

"I can't believe you just said that." Laurie whispered as tears clouded her eyes.

"Sorry," Miranda whispered, "I didn't mean it."

"Talking again!" boomed the deputy's voice, as he strode past several other lockers toward Miranda and Laurie. "Empty your pockets!"

"There's nothing in my pockets," Miranda replied, evenly.

"Don't give me any back talk! Reach in there and pull your pockets inside out or I will!"

He held her arm and reached into her front jeans pocket.

"Stop it!" Miranda screamed, jerking away.

She spun out of his grasp and ran toward the front office as he made another grab for her.

"Stop that girl!" he yelled as she sped by the sheriff who was searching a row of highschool kids.

She didn't look back. Reaching the office, she found the door locked. At the sound of footsteps pounding behind her, she pushed through the front door, ran across the road, dropped into tall brown grass, and lay perfectly still.

"What are you doing, Simmons? Get back in here!" Miranda heard the sheriff say.

Miranda lifted her head slowly and saw the deputy turn and go inside. She rose from the frozen ground, seething with anger until fear began to take its place. What would her parents and grandparents say about this new trouble she had gotten herself into? Well, she wasn't about to go back into the school! She'd walk home and tell her parents what happened before someone else did. At least she hoped so.

Grandma was on her way to get the cows in for milking by the time Miranda got home.

"Wait up, Gram. I'll go with you as soon as I grab a coat."

Her jacket was still in the schoolhouse, and though she had kept up a vigorous walk, running part of the way, Miranda was freezing. Her winter parka was hanging in her grandparents' back porch.

"I can hardly believe my ears, Miranda! Nothing like this has ever happened at Country View before. I wonder what it's all about," Grandma said after listening to Miranda's story. "Whatever it is, that young man was out of line! You won't be going back to school until we get an explanation and an apology!"

"Thanks for believing me, Grandma," Miranda said, as tears of relief stung her eyes. "Maybe I shouldn't have run away, but I was scared. I told him there was nothing in my pockets, and that was the truth. I wasn't trying to sass him."

"He had no right to touch you, even if he thought you were lying!"

"Will you go with me to explain it to Mom?"

"Sure," Grandma said.

Miranda didn't go to school the next day. Dad stayed home in the morning until he got in touch with the principal. Then, he and Mom went to talk to him in person, while Miranda stayed with Kort and Kaden.

At 11:00 they came back and Dad took Miranda directly to Mr. Alderman's office.

"Miranda, I apologize, and the Sheriff apologizes," Mr. Alderman said. "We wanted to snuff out drug abuse in this school before it became a bigger problem. The idea was to instill enough fear that kids would think twice before getting involved. The sheriff brought a new deputy he just hired. He just moved here from Chicago. The sheriff had no intention of being rough on the kids. Just wanted to scare them a little, while they searched lockers for drugs."

"Did they find any?" Miranda asked.

"No," Mr. Alderman said with a sigh. "Do you know of anyone bringing marijuana to school?"

"No," Miranda answered quickly. Her face reddened as if to belie her declaration.

"It's for the good of the school that we stop the spread of illegal drugs," Mr. Alderman said, eyeing her suspiciously. "I trust you will let me know if you see or hear anything. You'd be doing the students and all of us a favor."

"May I go to class now?" Miranda asked.

"You may. And again, I apologize for how you were treated."

In the hallway, Dad pulled her aside.

"Miranda, look at me. Do you know something

you aren't telling?"

"Dad, I've never seen drugs in school and I don't know if there are any or not."

"Honest?"

"Honest."

"But you know more than you're telling me, don't you?"

"Dad, can we talk about this later?" Miranda said as elementary students streamed by on their way to the lunchroom.

Dad glanced at them.

"Sure. Go on to class. Come to Shady Hills after school. I'll see you there."

Miranda slid into the desk next to Laurie as she entered Mrs. Whitman's classroom. Laurie turned her head away, leaned on her hand with elbow on desk, letting her soft brown curls fall like a curtain between them.

Miranda scribbled a note and pushed it in front of Laurie. Laurie picked it up and crumpled it into her fist without reading it. Rising from her seat, she went to the wastebasket and dropped it in.

"Hi, Chris, may I sit here?" Miranda asked at lunch time as she approached a table with her food tray.

"It's a free country," Chris said without looking up.

"I felt bad when the deputy was so mean to you in front of everyone. Did you get your knife back?"

"What's it to you?" Chris growled.

"I care. I felt sorry for you," Miranda stammered.

"Well don't! The last thing I need is the pity of a traitor!"

"Traitor? What are you talking about?"

"Don't act innocent! I heard about you getting stoned at Tammy's party. Now you want to blame it all on Laurie's cousin, so you come out smelling like a rose. You think you can get her kicked out of school and still have any friends left?"

"I'm not trying to get her kicked out!"

"That's not the way I heard it," Chris said, picking up his tray. He moved to another table. Miranda emptied her tray of untouched food and left the lunchroom.

Miranda was saddling Starlight when her Dad appeared at the stable door.

"Kind of cold to go riding, isn't it?" he asked.

"I don't mind the cold," she replied.

"We need to talk, Miranda. I've had the feeling lately that something's been troubling you. Please confide in me," Dad said in his most sympathetic voice. "What happened at Tammy's party that upset you? Did it have anything to do with what went on at school yesterday?"

Miranda could not hold back the tears when her Dad came in and put his arm around her.

"I can't tell, Dad. I want to because I know I'd feel better. But I can't get anyone in trouble."

"Then just tell me about your involvement without naming anyone else."

"I'm so sorry for what I did that night. I truly learned my lesson and will never, ever try it again, I promise," Miranda said between sobs.

"I believe you, Mandy, but what was it? Please."

"I tried marijuana. It was horrible. It made me sick and sad and, and, I just felt so weird. I don't know how anyone can like it."

"I'm sorry you had to experience that. I'm afraid some kids will become users. I hope it can be stopped before anyone gets hurt."

"Don't ask me who it was, Dad," Miranda said. "You know I can't tell."

"I'm guessing it's someone new at school this year," Dad said. "Was it Dennis?"

"No fair, Dad!" Miranda exclaimed, pulling away. "You said I didn't have to name any names!"

"You're right. I'm sorry. I was out of line."

Miranda took Starlight to the river pasture, riding in the shelter of the trees. Her toes were soon aching with cold. She cried over the loss of her two best friends. Why did they think she told on Rose Marie? She wished she could take back the mean words she had said. Still, Laurie should know she wouldn't tell on her cousin.

"Starlight, you're the only friend I have left. But I'm freezing. Let's get out of this wind."

Before school began the next morning, Miranda tried to find Laurie. She was determined to make Laurie listen to her and accept her apology. After searching the hallway and Mr. Carson's room, Miranda went to the sixth grade classroom where Laurie's dad taught.

"Don't play cat and mouse games with me, Rose Marie," Mr. Langley said in a low voice as Miranda approached the doorway.

Rose Marie slouched in the chair in front of Mr. Langley's desk.

"I've heard enough rumors about the raid to know you have something to do with it. I also heard that you took drugs to Tammy's party!" Mr. Langley exclaimed. "If this is true, I'm very disappointed that you'd betray our trust in you."

"Who told you that?" Rose Marie snarled. "I bet it was that snooty Miranda Stevens. She thinks she's so much better than everyone else. When Laurie hears how her precious friend is spreading rumors about me, she'll never speak to her again!"

Chapter Eleven

Miranda backed away from the doorway, stunned. It had been a long time since she had heard hateful words said about her, and it hurt. Not that she cared what Rose Marie thought, but she couldn't stand the thought of losing Laurie's friendship. Miranda was late for class, but when she entered Mr. Carson's room, Laurie's desk was empty.

When school was finally over, Miranda slumped into her seat on the bus. She had to watch Kort and Kaden while Mom went to get a hair cut in the small beauty shop that Mrs. Carson had opened in her home. Miranda didn't know how she'd manage to entertain the boys when all she really wanted was to go to sleep and forget everything. She felt she was living in a nightmare, or else that the happy times had been a dream and she'd had the misfortune of waking up.

Stopping at the mailbox, she pulled out the contents and shuffled through it as she walked slowly to the house. Surprisingly, Margot had stomped past it instead of racing to get the mail first, as she usually did. A letter addressed to Miranda Stevens in neat bold letters caught her eye. It was from the Pennsylvania city where she had written to Adam Barber. She quickly tore it open.

Dear Miranda,

Thanks for your letter. You sound angry, but I'm used to that from you. You imply that I don't love Margot. You're wrong. I may not know how to show it and fatherhood has always scared me, but I do care about my daughter.

You say I can give her the happiness she deserves by giving her up for adoption. At first, I was furious at you and your father for suggesting that. After all she is my daughter. But after giving it a lot of thought, I decided you're right.

Have your parents send me papers to sign. Please give the enclosed letter to Margot. Adam

There was a folded piece of note paper, taped shut, with Margot's name on the outside of it. Miranda ran to share it with her soon-to-be real sister!

"Margot, may I come in?" Miranda said, tapping on the open door to Margot's room.

Margot shrugged but didn't look her way.

"Look, Margot. I have proof that you're wanted in this family. You can stay forever. I want you to."

Margot finally looked up. Miranda was surprised to see a deep frown, angry eyes, and clenched jaw.

"Mar, what's the matter?"

Margot only shrugged and looked down.

"Please tell me."

"I don't think I want to be your sister," Margot began, as she stared at the floor.

"Why not? Margot. Talk to me!"

"Kids at school hate me. Everyone in my class was mean to me except Elliot."

"About what? Why?"

"They said it's your fault the cops came to school. They called you a big-fat-tattle-tale, and they wouldn't play with me because they think I'm your sister."

"Oh, no! I'm so sorry. They're treating me the same way, even Laurie and Chris who I thought would be my friends forever. I swear I didn't do anything. I don't know why they think I told. You've got to believe me, Margot!" Miranda exclaimed. "Elliot's still your friend, isn't he?"

"I don't know."

Margot pulled away when Miranda tried to hug her. Tears filled Miranda's eyes, but Margot didn't cry.

"Oh, Mar," Miranda exclaimed, "I almost forgot why I came in here. I got a letter from your Dad today. He's going to let us adopt you. I told you we wanted you in our family!"

"I knew he didn't love me. I should have known he'd be glad to give me away!" Margot said dismally.

"Good grief, Margot. I thought you'd be happy!" Miranda said. "I don't think it's like that. Here. I'm sure this letter will explain."

Margot turned the letter over and over, but didn't

remove the tape.

"Aren't you going to read it?" Miranda asked.

"I'll read it later . . . when I'm alone."

"Okay. I'll go. If you want to talk about it later, I'll be in my room."

Margot didn't come to her, however, and Miranda asked her after supper if she'd read it.

"Not yet," Margot said.

Miranda dreaded school every day. The longer her friends ignored her, the harder it became to get out of bed and drag herself to the bus. Laurie looked drawn and tired. Miranda tried to talk to her, but Laurie had little to say. Rose Marie, when she saw Miranda, either ignored her or spoke unkindly. Chris sat with Jody every lunch hour and failed to notice that Miranda existed. Dennis put his tray down across from Miranda one day soon after the raid, and Miranda looked up at him with a grateful smile. But Dennis didn't smile back.

"I got called into the office this morning and raked over the coals," he said. "No one would say why, but it was pretty easy to figure out from their questions that you told them I was responsible for the drugs at Tammy's party. I don't know what your trip is! First you finger Rose Marie; now me!"

"Dennis, I swear! I never told anyone anything. You didn't bring them! Why would I lie?"

"That's what I'd like to know."

"I didn't! And I never told on anyone and I don't know why people think I did," Miranda said.

But Dennis had already turned his back, taking his tray to another table.

"Did you tell the school that I said Dennis brought drugs to Tammy's party?" Miranda asked her father accusingly.

"No, I didn't tell the school anything. Why?"

Miranda told him what Dennis had said.

"No, Miranda. I hope you know me better than that. I wouldn't betray your confidence even if you had told me it was Dennis. And you didn't."

"I wish I never had to go back to school. I want to be home-schooled. Mom can teach me and that way I can help her more with the boys, and I can go with Mr. Taylor on racing tours," Miranda said, warming up to the subject. "This is a good idea, Dad!"

"No, it isn't."

"Why not?"

"Because you would be doing it for all the wrong reasons," he said. "You would be giving up."

There was a light in the dairy barn when they got home that night, and Miranda went to help Grandpa, pouring out her lament to him as she helped him finish up.

"Maybe you could talk Mom and Dad into letting me do home-study," she said.

"You can't run away from trouble, Mandy," Grandpa said. "This will blow over and the truth will reveal itself. When they all realize they wrongfully accused you, they'll want to be your friends again."

"I hope you're right, Grandpa."

It was only a week before Christmas vacation when Mrs. Bell stopped Miranda in the hallway.

"Miranda, I need to speak to you. Please walk with me to the music room if you have a minute,"

Miranda followed Mrs. Bell, wondering what she was in trouble for this time. Were the teachers going to gang up on her too? But it was lunch hour, none of her classmates were speaking to her, so she had nothing else to do.

"As you know, your friend Laurie has been out of school for a couple of days. I just got a call from her mother. Laurie has strept throat, bronchitis, and laryngitis!" Mrs. Bell said, as she sat on the piano bench and looked into Miranda's eyes.

"Oh, I'm sorry," Miranda said, wondering why Mrs. Bell wanted to tell her this privately.

"The Christmas program is Thursday night. Of the three numbers the chorus is planning, one is an exquisitely beautiful piece with a long solo. Laurie is our soloist, but there is no way that she will be able to sing. I've heard your voice, Miranda. Would you consider taking Laurie's place?"

"I, uh, I don't know. I don't even know the song," Miranda stammered.

"If you meet with me every lunch hour, we can practice for almost an hour each day on the solo. I can get you out of woodworking for the rest of the week so you can join chorus to learn the other songs."

"I don't know. I like to sing, but I'm not used to performing in front of an audience."

"You'll do fine! What do you say? I'll bring lunch for both of us."

The school Christmas program was a big deal. Not only did relatives of all the students, Kindergarten through high school, come, but other community members as well. Miranda, who already felt self-conscious in the long black skirt and white blouse that Mrs. Bell had asked her to wear, felt butterflies in her stomach as she saw the full auditorium. The lunch hours with Mrs. Bell had been like paradise. Miranda never dreamed she'd have so much fun singing. Mrs. Bell's creative lunches were a delight, and the enthusiasm with which the music teacher praised her lightened Miranda's heavy heart. Now she was having second thoughts. Would she be able to sing in front of this crowd? The hardest part was singing in front of her classmates. They would be her worst critics.

Miranda was on her way to meet the rest of the choir when Laurie stepped in front of her. Laurie was wearing a long black skirt and white blouse.

"What are you doing?" Laurie asked, eying Miranda's dress.

"I'm singing with the choir," Miranda said.

"Since when?" It sounded like an accusation.

"Since Mrs. Bell asked me. You were sick for so long, so . . . "

"So you think you can step in and take my

place?" Laurie demanded.

"But you have a cold!"

"I'm feeling better! I'm going to sing!" Laurie turned and marched toward the stage.

Miranda was bewildered. Tears blurred her vision and she started to follow Laurie. Changing her mind she slipped in beside Grandpa who sat in a row near the back. He hadn't finished the chores early enough to get a seat up front.

"What are you doing?" Grandpa asked.

"I don't have to sing after all," Miranda whispered. "Laurie's back."

"Did Mrs. Bell tell you she didn't need you?"

"No, but Laurie . . .,"

"You go find Mrs. Bell, and don't come back here unless she says she doesn't want you!"

Miranda hurried to the front of the gym where Mrs. Bell was giving last minute instructions.

"Miranda, there you are! I was told you weren't coming. Thank goodness you made it!"

Miranda stared at Laurie, who quickly looked away. Her friend had lied about her! Some friend. Miranda's anger boiled.

"Laurie, let's hear you run through the scale. I don't know if you should be straining your voice."

Mrs. Bell hit a note on the piano. Laurie trilled up and down the scale, but her voice caught on a high note, and she began to cough.

"If you really want, you may join us, but if your voice plays out, just lip sync. Miranda is going to do the solo, so you don't have to worry." Turning to Miranda, Mrs. Bell asked, "Are you ready?"

Miranda's emotions were in such turmoil she didn't know if she could make a sound. It would have been much easier if Laurie hadn't shown up. The rest of the small choir had seemingly accepted her, but from their menacing glances, Miranda sensed they were now on Laurie's side.

"Miranda," Mrs. Bell repeated. "Don't freeze up on me now. Remember what we talked about. Just think of the song. Forget everything and everyone else."

As they took their places on stage, Miranda, being tallest, had to stand in the middle with Laurie next to her. Mrs. Bell played the opening chords. Miranda opened her mouth to sing, but her voice squeaked and she stopped.

Chapter Twelve

Miranda's face burned as the others went on, some sounding off key and breathless. She took a deep breath. She had to get her composure before the last song, which was mostly her solo. *Think of something else. Don't let Laurie get to you,* Miranda told herself. Laurie was carrying the melody until she reached for a high note. Her voice broke, and the others faltered. There was an embarrassing silence as the piano went on without them. Mrs. Bell stopped, stood, smiled at the audience, and then faced the choir.

"Don't be afraid," she whispered, "Those people out there are going to love you no matter how you sing. Just have fun with it like we do in the classroom. Okay? We'll start over."

"Sing, Miranda," Laurie hissed as Mrs. Bell went back to the piano.

I guess it doesn't matter what I do, there's no pleasing Laurie. Miranda looked at the audience and smiled.

"Miranda, that was beautiful," her mother said hugging her when the program was over. "You sing like an angel!"

"I can't remember when I've heard such a pure, sweet voice!" exclaimed a woman Miranda didn't know, as the crowd mingled in the back of the gym

after the program.

"Good job," said another stranger. "You have a special talent."

"Daughter, you continue to surprise me," Dad said, "I hope you'll keep singing with the chorus now. You can switch from woodworking second semester."

"I knew you could do it, Mandy!" Grandpa said, squeezing her hand. "I've heard you sing to the cows and calves."

Miranda left with Mr. Taylor, Colton, and Grandma, the next day. Once again, the family would be separated on Christmas, but they had all agreed to postpone their traditional celebration until New Year's Eve when they would all be together again. Until Grandma had suggested that she go along, Mom had strongly opposed letting Miranda go. Miranda was grateful. It would be fun having Gram along. Best of all, she would be with Starlight.

The Taylor ranch in southeastern Texas, where Miranda stayed the year before, had been sold, so they drove straight to Sam Houston Race Park, in Houston. Colton and Mr. Taylor would stay in the living quarters of the horse van, and Grandma and Miranda had reservations in a nearby hotel.

Miranda rode Starlight around the track before post time. He was in perfect health and eager to run.

"Hold on, boy. It's not time yet to show everyone what you can do. Save the surprise for when Colton rides you in the first race."

When the race was announced, Miranda mounted Mr. Taylor's old gelding, as Colton got a boost onto Starlight. Taking the lead rope, Miranda rode around the track with the rest of the entrants. It was traditional to have someone lead the race horses and their jockeys once around the track before loading into the starting gate. Mr. Taylor believed it was an advantage to have Miranda doing the leading, hoping it would convey the message to Starlight that he would be running for his mistress, the one person he lived to please.

"He's loving every minute of this," Miranda said to Colton. "I don't think you'll have any trouble with him if you just do what we always do."

"I hope not. I can't take much more criticism from old man Taylor," Colton replied. "If I don't win, I'll sure hear how it was all my fault."

"That's just Mr. Taylor's way. He doesn't really mean it. Don't pay any attention to him."

"That's easy for you to say. I've been waiting for an apology for the time he reamed me out for being swatted in the face. It will never come, of course," Colton growled.

"Don't worry, Colton. You're going to win. And if Mr. Taylor doesn't like the way you ride, just tell him you can get a job for someone else. I think you're the best rider in the field."

"Thanks, Miranda. I wish he thought so."

"He probably does. He just doesn't say it."

Miranda joined Grandma and Mr. Taylor in the

stands after leading Starlight to the gate. Another horse was balking so she had time to get settled before the race began. Starlight leapt from the gate as it opened and was a length ahead of the pack by the time they raced past them.

"I wish he'd hold him back just a little in the beginning," Mr. Taylor said.

"You know that doesn't work with Starlight. He fights if you pull back on him," Miranda reminded Mr. Taylor.

Starlight began to slow a little and look sideways. Miranda had seen this before. He was waiting for the other horses to catch up. As soon as they did, he matched their speed, but didn't pull ahead by more than a neck. Colton sat relaxed, weight back in his saddle, just as Miranda would have done if she had been riding. In the backstretch, the rider in second place began whipping his horse with a crop and it surged ahead of Starlight. Colton leaned over Starlight's ears, and Miranda knew just what he was saying. "Okay, boy. It's time to go. Go, Go, Go!"

And Starlight went. Lengthening his stride, he powered ahead, crossing the finish line a length ahead of the horses that finished a close second and third. Mr. Taylor was elated.

"I knew he could do it. That was perfect. He didn't win by so much that he gave our hand away, but it got us the purse."

Miranda sped to the winner's circle.

"Way to go, Colton!" she yelled, as she took

Starlight's reins. "Good boy, Starlight. You were perfect."

As they walked back to the stables, Mr. Taylor exuberantly sang Starlight's praises. At last he paused and added, "If you wait just a little longer before pouring on the coals, Colton, it would be better. If we win by a nose this afternoon, people will think he's tiring and will still bet against him in the races tomorrow. The more we can surprise them, the better my odds."

"See what I mean?" Colton grumbled, as he and Miranda unsaddled Starlight. "He never once gave me any credit for winning. Just told me how I could do it better. That old man is impossible to please."

In the afternoon race, Colton did his best to follow Mr. Taylor's orders. He waited until they were almost to the finish line before giving Starlight the go ahead. Two horses were in front of him. Starlight burst forward, but came in so close that it was called a photo finish. Waiting with Mr. Taylor was driving Miranda crazy. The old man accused Colton of trying to give him a heart attack by not just winning outright. If they were only second, he would lose money on his bets.

Colton clenched his jaw, biting back words as his face reddened. But then the results came in.

"Sir Jet Propelled Cadillac, otherwise known as Starlight, is first. Maybelline Marcello is second."

"Wahoo!" Mr. Taylor exclaimed. "We did it. What a horse! It turned out okay, Colton. In fact it couldn't be better."

"See, Colton, Mr. Taylor thought you were great once he got over being scared he'd lost a lot of money."

Miranda said when they were alone.

"That doesn't mean a thing, Miranda. You know that. If we'd lost the photo, he would have blamed me. And didn't you notice? He never said I did anything right, just that it turned out okay. A thank you would have been nice."

"But that's just Mr. Taylor. He's a natural grouch, Colton. Sure, he should say thank you, but if you don't tell him so, he won't think of it. I don't think he means to be so hard on you," Miranda said.

"So you're on his side. Well, I'm not going to go telling him I want a thank you. If he doesn't appreciate my work, I'll find someone who will."

"I'm not against you, Colton. I think you're the greatest. I think Mr. Taylor should tell you so and double your pay, but he probably won't. I was just saying don't take it so personal."

"It is personal," Colton said as he walked away.

On the day before Christmas, Starlight was scheduled for one race. Colton was obviously nervous when he approached the starting gate. Sensing his fear, Starlight stomped and tossed his head nervously.

"Easy, boy. It's just another race. Just do what you always do," Miranda said as she patted Starlight's muzzle. "Colton, relax. You'll do fine."

"I don't even know what the old man wants me to do. Am I supposed to let Starlight win by a sweep, or hold him back for another close one? That's the hardest and I'm dead meat if I lose."

"Forget what he wants. Starlight will win. It's

not your fault that Mr. Taylor gambles on his horses."

No sooner had Miranda reached the edge of the track than the gates opened. Miranda couldn't see Starlight very well, but something seemed to be wrong. As the other horses moved ahead, she saw Starlight crow-hopping across the track. Colton, wide eyed, was struggling to stay on.

"Starlight," she yelled. "Go, go, go!"

Looking ahead at the other horses, Starlight quit bucking and jumped forward, almost unseating Colton. He raced toward the others, quickly closing the gap. Miranda was peering through the fence when the pack entered the backstretch. Starlight had passed the others and slowed, as if inviting them to catch him. When they did, Colton leaned over his withers and began talking to him. Starlight seemed to ignore him and let three horses go on by. Now in the home stretch, Starlight was in fourth place with another horse coming up on the inside.

"Go, Starlight, GO!" Miranda screamed.

He sped forward, his powerful strides pulling him ahead of the horse on the rail, then past the third position. He was catching up with the horse in second as they crossed the finish line.

"Clairvoyant wins by half a length," the announcer yelled. "We'll have to wait for a photo to announce second and third."

"Shoot! Miranda. What happened? Starlight did whatever he wanted as if I wasn't even there. Maybe Mr. Taylor's right!" Colton exclaimed as he swung off.

"What got him bucking out of the gate?" Miranda asked.

"I don't know. He jumped and put his ears back before the gate even opened," Colton said, frowning. "Whatever it was, I'll be blamed. If he yells at me, I quit!"

"Look. Someone stuck a pin in his rump. Poor boy! Miranda said, pulling a hat pin from Starlight's hip. "That explains it. Now Mr. Taylor can't be mad at you."

"Darn cheaters!" Colton shouted. "No wonder he acted up!"

"I'm going to find out who did it!" Miranda said.

"There's no way, Miranda. No one will ever admit it. We could go to the racing commission and tell, but they wouldn't do anything. Just tell Mr. Taylor and let him take care of it."

However, Mr. Taylor surprised them both by staying away.

Miranda didn't see him until the next morning when they all got together for breakfast at the restaurant next to the motel. It was a very quiet meal as the tension ran high, and Grandma's attempts at small talk were met with mere grunts.

"I've got some people to see today. You three spend Christmas however you want to. I'll see you tomorrow," Mr. Taylor grunted as he stood to leave.

"What a relief not to have to be around him all day," Colton said. "He hasn't said two words to me since yesterday's race. I don't think he believed me when I told him someone had jammed a needle into him."

"I'll tell him when I see him tomorrow. Maybe he'll listen to me," Miranda said.

"No," Colton said. "I'm not having a girl fight my battles."

Grandma invited Colton to go with her and Miranda to see some of the sights of Houston. They went to the zoo, the Museum of Natural Science, and the downtown aquarium. They ate dinner at a Chinese restaurant. Colton had never eaten Chinese food before and declared it his favorite.

"My dad told me I wouldn't like it, because he didn't, so I never tasted it," he said. "It just goes to show you can't let other people think for you."

"That's a good lesson," Grandma said with a chuckle. "It's nice we can learn from something as simple as Chinese cuisine."

"Let's see what we can learn from a Chinese fortune," Miranda said, picking up one of the three fortune cookies the waitress placed on the table. "Mine says, 'You will find fame and fortune in unexpected twists of fate.' Hmm, well at least I'm going to have fame and fortune," she said, laughing.

"How do you know that cookie wasn't supposed to be mine or your Grandma's?" Colton asked, picking up another cookie.

"I guess which ever one you pick is yours. It's part of the fortune game, don't you think?"

"Could be," Grandma said, "but I wouldn't place too much stake on a fortune cookie, no matter which one you happen to pick up."

"You have an important decision to make regarding your future," Colton read. "Well, that sounds right."

"Read yours, Gram," Miranda urged.

"Your true love is thinking of you today," Grandma said. With a twinkle in her eye, she added, "Well, who do you suppose that would be?"

"Grandpa, of course. But that didn't tell you anything. He thinks of you all the time."

As Miranda, riding Mr. Taylor's gelding, Pecos, led Starlight from the stables for their procession around the track, Mr. Taylor finally appeared.

"Uh oh. Here it comes," Colton said.

As they stopped in front of the old man, he looked up at Colton.

"I don't want any more of your shenanigans on the track today, Colton. Just ride like Miranda taught you to and let Starlight win!" He turned and started walking away.

"Taylor!" Colton shouted. "If you don't like my 'shenanigans,' get another jockey. I'm done."

Colton dismounted and pulled off the vest with his number, and his Shady Hills jersey, thrusting them at Mr. Taylor.

"What are you doing? Get back on that horse!" Mr. Taylor ordered.

"No way. I've listened to the last scolding I ever want to hear from you. I quit!"

Chapter Thirteen

Mr. Taylor stared after Colton in astonishment and then looked at the jersey and vest in his arms.

"The race is about to start," he yelled. "Come back here and finish your job!"

Colton didn't turn around, but kept walking, shirtless, toward the trailer.

"I don't think he's going to come back," Miranda said. "You've been awfully hard on him, and he's been doing his best. You'll have a hard time finding a better rider."

"Well, I'm not giving up on this race. I have too much at stake. Miranda, run to the trailer, grab your helmet, and put these on. Make it fast and I'll pony you around the track. Hurry."

"But Mr. Taylor, I'm not certified. I'm not old enough, and besides, I'd have to ask Grandma first."

"There's no time. Do as I say. I'll explain everything to your grandmother. No one else will know it's not Colton. Tuck your hair up under the helmet."

Exhilarated by the realization that she was riding in an actual race, Miranda grinned broadly as she guided Starlight into the starting gate. *Another dream come true,* she thought. But her smile faded as she realized that what she was doing was not only illegal, but in complete violation of her family's wishes. *Would Grandma ever be mad! But,* she thought, *it's not my fault. I'm just obeying Mr. Taylor.* The thought was not entirely comforting.

Miranda grabbed leather as the power of Starlight's forward thrust nearly unbalanced her. They were off and in the lead. She let Starlight run without urging him or pulling him in. Transported to an ethereal realm of unbelievable joy, Miranda felt, as she always did when she raced Starlight, that she and he were one being. Nothing else existed but the two of them. No trouble in the world could touch her as long as they ran together.

Starlight slowed slightly and looked to his left and then his right.

"You're waiting for them, aren't you boy. Well, that's fine. Play all you want. You can beat any horse on the planet without half trying."

Pain shot through her right foot and a blow to her elbow threw her off balance. She held on and righted herself. She glimpsed the horse and rider that were scraping by her. A chunk of mud hit her in the face as another horse passed on the left. She winced and closed her eyes, frightened. She stood in the stirrups and leaned over Starlight's neck.

"Get me out of here, boy!" She said, "Go, Starlight!"

The response was immediate. When he surged ahead of the others, Miranda breathed a sigh of relief and relaxed a little. As Starlight slowed, she leaned over his neck.

"Just stay ahead, okay? I'm not ready to fight the crowd."

Starlight did as she asked, keeping up the pace all the way around the track. When she came into the homestretch, even though there were no other horses within her peripheral vision, she leaned forward and spoke into his ears again. "Now Starlight, pour it on, GO! GO! GO!"

They swept across the finish line to the roar of the crowd.

"Sir Jet Propelled Cadillac has won by at least six lengths. Can you believe it, folks? This horse has left the rest of the pack so far in the dust, they didn't know he was in the race!" the announcer shouted over the public address system.

As Miranda came around the track the second time, a crowd of people was storming the track including reporters with cameras and microphones. She looked frantically around for Mr. Taylor, but couldn't see him in the crowd. As she rode toward the winner's circle, microphones were thrust in her face.

"Mr. Spencer, how do you account for today's performance?" "Has he ever run like this before?" "Were you holding him back in the previous races this week? If so, why did you let him run today?"

Miranda shook her head and urged Starlight to move through the crowd, but someone held his rein. Miranda looked helplessly around for Mr. Taylor. He was accosted by a reporter, too.

"No comment!" she heard him yell. "Get away, you're upsetting the horse. He's not used to this kind of commotion."

Starlight, however, didn't seem the least bit upset, but stood, head high, surveying the crowd.

"Mr. Spencer, how would you compare this horse with other's you have ridden," a reporter insisted, "Answer me, Colton. How do you feel about this win?"

"Let me through!" Miranda's voice squeaked with fear, though she meant to sound like Colton.

"Wait! Who are you?" one reporter yelled.

"That's not Colton Spencer!" another said.

Hands snatched at her feet and legs.

"It's just a kid!" someone shouted, dragging her from Starlight's back.

"Stop it! Let me go," she shouted.

Starlight swung his head toward Miranda, knocking a reporter to the ground.

Another hand pulled the helmet from her head, choking her and scratching her chin with the buckle. Her long blond hair tumbled to her shoulders.

"Aha! It's a girl," a man said, poking a microphone at her face. "What's your name? What happened to Colton Spencer?"

"Mr. Taylor will explain. I just want to take Starlight back to the stable. Please," Miranda begged.

"Clear the track, people. We have a race waiting to start. Get out of the track before we get a swat team in here!" The announcer shouted over the P.A. "I mean it people. We can't keep these horses in the gates any longer. Get out of the way or you'll be trampled."

The crowd cleared enough for Miranda to move. Holding Starlight's reins, she ran from the track, Starlight trotting behind her. Mr. Taylor intercepted her at the alleyway that led to the stables.

"Gosh darn it all, Miranda. Why did you have to run away like that? After all I've been telling Colton about keeping the lead small, I thought you'd have the sense to do the same," Mr. Taylor scolded. "Now look at the pickle I'm in."

"Sir Jet Propelled Cadillac, the winner of the last race, has been disqualified. His owner, Mr. Cassius Taylor of Shady Hills Horse Ranch in Montana will be fined for violating racing rules. The rider of Sir Jet was not Colton Spencer, as announced in your racing schedule, but, according to an unofficial source, a twelve-year-old girl named Miranda Stevens!"

The announcer's voice boomed loud and clear over the race park.

"I'm not twelve. I'm thirteen!" Miranda shouted, to no one in particular.

"And you are in more trouble than you can possibly imagine," said Grandma, pushing through the crowd. "Mr. Taylor, I want an explanation. Why was my granddaughter on that horse in the middle of a professional race? She could have been killed!"

The trip back to Montana was long, boring, and tense. Grandma was angry with both Miranda and Mr. Taylor. Miranda had pled that she had no choice. Mr. Taylor had told her to ride.

"You always have a choice, Miranda. If someone told you to jump off a cliff to certain death, would you do it?" Grandma asked. "I don't care who it is. If someone asks you to do something you know is wrong, don't do it. If you need someone to back you up come to me, but you don't ever have to do anything against your own conscience."

Mr. Taylor was still mad at her, too. She had never gotten the chance to defend herself for drawing so much attention by winning by such an unbelievable distance. But what could she say? "I got scared?" "I couldn't stand being pinned in by other riders so I just wanted to get away and stay ahead?" That would be admitting that she was a coward. She wished she had kept her head and run the way she always advised Colton to, but it all happened so fast.

Miranda missed Colton. The ride to Texas had been much more fun because Colton had played games with her, anything she suggested. They had played the alphabet game when they went through towns where they could find letters on signs. They looked for pictures in the clouds, and Miranda was surprised that Colton had an imagination even greater than her own. They'd played rhyming games and I Spy with Grandma often joining in. But today a gloom that seemed to forbid talk or laughter settled over the three travelers. She wondered where Colton was right now.

"Sorry I yelled at you, Miranda," Mr. Taylor said, finally breaking a four-hour-long silence. "It was wrong of me to ask you to ride, and I had no call to raise my voice at you."

"Why did you?" Grandma asked as Miranda struggled to think of an answer.

"Just like with Colton. I got myself in a pickle and took it out on him. I knew I was done for when they discovered I had switched jockeys. Especially with her being underage."

"I mean why did you let her ride? Didn't you realize you were risking her life?" Grandma asked.

"No, actually I didn't. I've seen her do such wonders with that horse so many times, that it never occurred to me that she might have trouble in the race."

"Then you weren't thinking very straight!" Grandma accused.

"That's what I'm saying. I used poor judgment, and all because I got myself into a bind. I lost over three million dollars on the race alone besides the fine I still have to pay," Mr. Taylor said sadly as he stared down the highway.

"How could you lose so much?" Grandma asked.

"Gambling. The more I win, the more I believe I can win, the more I bet." After a pause, he continued with a sidelong glance at Miranda. "Let that be a lesson to you, girl. Never start gambling. It's a hard habit to break."

"Three million dollars!" Miranda exclaimed with a low whistle. "How are you going to pay it?"

"I don't know," he sighed. "I may lose Shady Hills just like I lost my parents' ranch; selling it to pay off gambling debts. But there is one upside to the way you won the race today. Starlight is suddenly worth more money. I was offered 500,000, and I just laughed at the guy. Another man offered twice that."

"Mr. Taylor! You can't sell him. He's half mine. Please say you will never sell him!"

Mr. Taylor only grunted and his knuckles whitened as he gripped the steering wheel.

"Whose car is that in the driveway?" Miranda asked as Mr. Taylor let them off at the gate to Greene's dairy just after midnight the next day.

"I don't know," Grandma said. "Looks like we have company from out of state."

A dog howled from the shed as they approached Grandma's house.

"Do you want me to walk you to your house?" Grandma asked.

"No, that's all right. There's plenty of moonlight and I'll let the dogs out of the shed to go with me." Miranda said.

Miranda patted Little Brother, as he jumped up on her, nearly knocking her down.

"You big oaf," she laughed. "I'm glad to see you too. Tell you what, I'll let you sleep with me if you promise to be quiet."

Miranda tiptoed to her room, shushing Little Brother when he growled. She sat on the edge of the bed and took off her shoes. She didn't turn a light on, deciding she just wanted to fall into bed and go to sleep.

"C'mon, Little Brother," she said to the hundred

thirty-five pound Labrador/Newfoundland cross. "Jump up here."

She patted the bed and felt a large form under the covers. It moved. Stifling a scream, Miranda stumbled to the doorway and flipped on the overhead light. Adam Barber sat up in her bed, squinting at her. Miranda yelped.

"My gosh, what on earth are you doing here?" You about gave me a heart attack!"

"I'm sorry. You weren't expected until tomorrow or the next day," Adam stammered, looking as surprised as she was. "Carey told me to sleep in here."

"Sorry. I didn't know. I'll sleep on the couch."

"No, you can have your bed. Just leave long enough for me to get some clothes on. I'll take the couch."

Miranda picked up her suitcase where she had dropped it by the bed.

"I have a better idea. Little Brother and I will sleep with Margot. I don't think you'd fit on the couch."

"Miranda, you're home!" Mom exclaimed as Miranda stepped out of her room.

Miranda hugged her mother. Sleepy-eyed and yawning, Margot joined them in the hallway.

"I didn't know you were coming yet," Margot said. "Is everything okay?"

"Welcome home, traveler," said Dad.

The lusty cries of a hungry baby interrupted her reply.

"Oh, no! He'll wake Kort!" Mom said hurrying

to lift Kaden from his crib.

"Too late," Miranda said, as she watched Kort slide out of his youth bed in the nursery and walk toward her rubbing his eyes.

"Manda! Now we can open presents!" Kort exclaimed, holding his arms out to her.

"Can we? Everyone is awake," Margot said, as Miranda held Kort in a big hug.

"Hold on," Dad said, laughing. "Let's all sit around the tree while Mom feeds Kaden. I'll make hot chocolate, and Miranda can tell us all about her trip."

"Open presents," Kort insisted, getting down from Miranda's arms and running to the tree.

"No, Kort," Margot said.

"Oh, let him have one. He's been waiting a long time. We told him he could open them when Miranda got home. To him, that means now." Mom said.

"When did Adam get here?" Miranda asked Margot when they finally got into bed.

"Just today. It's weird. I kept wishing you would get home."

"Did you ever read the letter he sent?"

Margot shook her head sheepishly and opened the top drawer of her desk.

"Let's read it together," she said.

"Why didn't you read it?"

"I was afraid I wouldn't like what it said. And then I didn't know what I wanted it to say, and wasn't sure I'd believe it. If it said he loved me and was just doing the best for me, then I wouldn't believe it, and if he said he didn't want me, my feelings would be hurt, and if he said he wanted me to come live with him and made promises to be a better Dad, I wouldn't know what to do, so I just never read it."

Dear Margot,

I've told Barry and Carey Stevens that they may adopt you if that's what you want. I don't know how I feel about it. Guilty, I guess, for not being a better father to you. It's not that I don't love you. I do. You may find that hard to believe, but it's true. However, I'm not good with kids and I'll be the first to admit it. Even though I've decided to let them adopt you, I don't want you to forget me, and I won't forget you. I want to start communicating more, visiting more, so we can get to know each other. But in the meantime I think the Stevens can give you a secure and safe home. If it's what you want, let's go ahead and make it official. If it's not, you can tell me when I come to visit after Christmas.

Love, Dad, or Adam or whatever you want to call me.

The remaining three days of Christmas vacation

passed all too quickly. There was so much to catch up on. To Miranda's surprise, Adam's visit was actually pleasant. He was kind to Margot and, miracle of miracles, apologized to Miranda for being so bossy and rude to her in the past. After all the documents were in order and signed by the judge, there was a party at home with a huge cake that said, *Margot Stevens, Welcome to the Family!* Mom, Dad, and Miranda signed it in bright colored icing. Mom helped Kort write his name, and wrote Kaden's too.

"Cut the cake, Margot," Miranda said, handing her a silver cake knife with a purple bow tied around it.

Margot took the knife, looked at everyone, whispered, "Thanks," then burst into tears and ran to her bedroom.

Chapter Fourteen

Miranda looked at the rest of the family wondering what had happened. They all seemed as baffled as she was. They crowded together outside Margot's bedroom door. Miranda knocked, and tried to turn the knob. It was locked. Adam knocked and asked if he could come in. No answer. Mom asked if she was okay, and would she like some company. Again, no answer.

"Mar, do you want to talk about it later or is there something someone can help with now?"

The door opened a crack and Margot whispered, "Just Miranda."

Miranda went in and closed the door. Tears drenched Margot's face. It was the first time Miranda had seen her cry for a long time.

"Don't think I'm a baby," Margot sobbed. "I don't know why I'm crying. I'm happy and everything, but sad too."

"It's okay, Mar. You know I cry at almost anything. It doesn't matter why. Cry when you feel like it and ask why later."

"B-b-but everyone will think . . . " Margot said between sobs.

"Oh, Margot! It doesn't matter. Everyone here loves you. If it'll make you feel better, I'll go tell them you're not mad. Do you want me to come back?"

Margot nodded.

It was far into the night when Margot finally quit sobbing, squeezed Miranda's hand, and fell into a sound, dreamless sleep.

Adam stayed a day longer than he intended thinking that Margot had changed her mind and was crying because he had given her up for adoption. That wasn't the case.

"I started to cry because I was happy. I was afraid to hope I would ever be a part of this family; afraid I wouldn't get to stay," Margot explained to Miranda the next morning. "But as soon as I started crying, I got all mixed up. I thought how Dad actually loves me and wants what's best for me. I don't have to be afraid of him anymore, and I actually feel love for him. But mostly I thought about Mom. My mother! I thought how she would be happy for me, and how much I miss her. And lots of the time I didn't think at all. I just couldn't stop crying."

If it hadn't been for chorus, Miranda didn't think

she could stand going to school. She had hoped that after being away, everything would be all right when she returned. It wasn't. Her heart had skipped a beat when she saw Laurie in the hallway near their lockers on the first day of school in January.

"Hi Laurie, I missed you," Miranda said. "Did you have a nice Christmas?"

Laurie seemed to freeze for a moment before looking at Miranda.

"It was okay," she said. "How was yours?"

"It was wild. I have so much to tell you. I got into so much trouble, you won't believe . . .," Miranda began.

"Miranda, it's not hard to believe you got into trouble. You always do. I've got to go to class now."

Laurie left without looking back and Miranda felt as if Laurie had slapped her. In fact, she wished she had. It would be easier to deal with than this invisible wall she felt between them.

The day did not improve and Miranda couldn't wait to get out of there and see Starlight. She didn't care how cold it was, they'd go for a long run in the river pasture — she'd ride until she was numb, but she'd be free from heartache, at least for those minutes she shared with Starlight.

Starlight seemed glad to be back on his own turf, but Miranda sensed a longing in him that she felt herself; the longing to run like the wind, to outrun everything in sight. If only she could ride him like that every day of the year. But the weather turned colder, so she rode in the indoor arena. But even that didn't last long, as her toes would begin hurting in less than an hour, no matter how many pairs of socks she wore.

She spent more time at home, playing with her sister and brothers and helping around the house. She took more responsibility for helping in the dairy because Grandpa's back hurt worse in the cold weather. She got

pretty good at putting milkers on the cows and making sure not to leave them on too long. She bucket fed calves, cleaned the machinery and the milking parlor, and kept an eye on heifers and cows that were getting close to calving. Of course, Grandma worked alongside her when Grandpa couldn't make it to the milk barn. Dad did the feeding morning and night. Margot helped take care of the chickens and rabbits.

At school, she spent her lunch hours with Mrs. Bell who was coaching her on a solo for the district music festival in the spring. It was Miranda's favorite time of day; an oasis of peace in the midst of the tension she felt from her classmates. Rose Marie was especially spiteful whenever they chanced to meet in the hallway.

Tears stung Miranda's eyes when she heard the cruel words, but she made up her mind to ignore them. What did she care what Rose Marie or her groupies thought? But she did care about Laurie, and it seemed Rose Marie had been successful in turning her against Miranda forever.

The weather eased, and in late February, a Chinook wind drove away the last snowstorm. The sun shone brightly on the rivulets of melting snow that creased the driveway and the roads. The cows churned the corrals into deep sloppy mud.

"Let's get ready for a sale," Grandpa said when Miranda, Dad, and Grandma entered the little farmhouse after finishing the chores one evening.

"What do you mean?" Grandma asked, sitting down at the table across from where Grandpa sat with a pile of papers and a calculator.

"It's time to retire, Kathy. And we can!" he exclaimed. "No more of this hard work for my girls, when I can't be out there helping."

"Are you going to sell this place?" Miranda asked in alarm.

"Oh no," Grandpa said. "I'll live right here until I die, but I'm getting too old to keep milking cows. My back has never been right since the accident. The pain takes all the fun out of milking."

"Fun?" Barry asked with a grin. "I don't think there's a lot of that in milking cows, but seriously, I can help out more and give Mom more time off."

"No, I know you don't care for the dairy business, Barry. And I've finally decided I'm not ever going to get over this bad back enough to work like I used to. We have a good retirement fund built up and this place is free and clear. I just want to sell the livestock, unless you want to take over the operation."

"No thanks. I just can't see myself milking cows for the rest of my life."

"What about you, Kathy? Do you think you can stand to let the cows go?"

"Of course, I can. I'm sure we'll miss it some, but we'll find plenty to do. Maybe we can get you the kind of treatment you need to feel good again."

It was decided that the sale would be held the first Saturday of March. They would auction off all the cattle and milking equipment as well as a lot of household goods, miscellaneous tools, and antiques that had accumulated over the years."

"It'll be nice to finally weed out some of the junk and have more room in the house and garage," Grandma said.

"After the sale, you can convert the dairy barn into a work shop if you want, Barry. I won't be using it anymore," Grandpa offered.

The sale was a big success, having been advertised in papers around the state. The day after the sale, Miranda went to Shady Hills. Preparing for the auction, on top of the extra chores she was doing at home, had kept her away far too long. Starlight seemed as glad to see her, as she was to see him. She rode him through the river pasture, over hills, and across open meadows.

"I wish Laurie and Chris were with us, Starlight. Do you miss Queen and Lady as much as I miss my friends?"

As she rode back to the stable, she saw Mr. Taylor standing beside the horse van, motioning the truck back toward the hitch. Dad was driving the truck.

"Going somewhere, Mr. Taylor?" She asked.

"Taking a few horses over to South Dakota. I'll leave bright and early tomorrow morning. A rancher's hosting a big horse sale. The nice thing about it is he's putting on an informal race ahead of time. If my horses show well they should bring a good price."

"Who are you taking?" Miranda asked, holding her breath.

"Sunny Side Up, Roman Candle, and a couple

others; probably Lady in Black Satin. I'd take Ebon's Dark Shadow if she wasn't about to foal."

"But these are your fastest horses!" Miranda exclaimed. "Why do you want to sell them?"

"Need the money, Miranda. I have to sell what will bring me the most."

"I think you and Miranda should prepare this piece for Festival as a duet, Laurie," Mrs. Bell said at the beginning of Chorus on Monday.

Laurie looked stunned as she took the sheet music Mrs. Bell was handing her.

"But it's so late!" Laurie argued. "We won't have time to get ready, besides, I'm already working on a trio."

"The way you two sing, I don't think you'll have any trouble polishing it up in a month's time. Come to the piano and we'll go over it a couple times before we work on the ensemble."

Miranda stepped up to the piano, her eyes on Laurie. Laurie looked down at the music. Stepping closer so that she could see it, Miranda took hold of one side of the paper. She noticed Laurie stiffen. As they began to sing, both girls gradually relaxed, even laughed over a mistake or two.

After class, Miranda said, "I'm glad we can sing together, Laurie. You have a beautiful voice." When Laurie didn't reply, she continued. "I'm going to Shady Hills after school. Want to come?"

"No, thanks," Laurie said shortly.

Miranda fought the empty feeling inside with thoughts of her horse, as she rode the bus to Shady Hills.

"Starlight," she called as she entered his stall. "Come here boy, we'll have some fun all by ourselves. Starlight?"

The stall was empty. She looked in his paddock. He wasn't there.

Chapter Fifteen

When Miranda called Dad at home, he said he didn't know where Starlight was. He hadn't worked that day because he was remodeling the milk barn. Miranda ran to ask Higgins, but he wasn't sure which horses Mr. Taylor had taken to South Dakota.

"Normally, I would have helped him load, but he was up and gone before I woke up," Higgins said sounding a little disappointed. "I think he knew I'd advise against some of his choices. I've never seen him so desperate for money. But no matter how low he may feel, I can't believe he'd take Starlight."

Miranda didn't share Higgins confidence in Mr. Taylor. She *knew* what had happened! He had said he was going to sell some of his most valuable horses and Starlight was his most valuable horse!

Under a gray sky and against a cold wind,

Miranda rushed around the ranch, looking into every stall, paddock, and nearby pasture. Though there were still many horses on the ranch, the number had diminished considerably since she first came to Shady Hills. Why would a person gamble away everything he had worked his whole life for? It was hard to understand.

"It's a disease, like alcoholism, or drug addiction," her father had told her. "A person with a compulsion to gamble never thinks he will lose. He only bets on 'sure things,' and when they turn out bad, the gambler tells himself the next time will be different. And when their gambling gets them into a financial bind, they try to solve it with more gambling."

When hope of finding Starlight diminished, tears stung her eyes and wet her cheeks. A snowflake landed on her nose and then more fell, blending with her tears. Miranda checked again on Queen and Lady. They had clean stalls, food, and water, though she knew that neither Chris nor Laurie had been there to take care of them. They must have asked Higgins to do it. That made her angry. Higgins was getting old and had more work than one person could possibly do. They ought to take care of their horses themselves. *Maybe they would if I wasn't here*. The thought only increased her flow of tears. She looked in on the weanlings and yearlings in the large paddock they shared. Some of them were Starlight's children; *the prettiest ones*, Miranda thought.

She went to see Ebon's Dark Shadow. She was in the sheltered corral by the barn where the door stood open so she could get in out of the weather. Her belly was huge with the baby growing inside her. As Miranda turned to leave, a movement in the barn door caught her eye. Sea Foam waddled toward her.

With surprise, Miranda noted that Sea Foam bulged more than Shadow did. She looked like she could foal any day, and Miranda hadn't even noticed she was pregnant. From a bag of carrots intended for Starlight, Miranda fed them one by one to the homely little horse. Sea Foam ate eagerly as Miranda examined her closely.

"Sea Foam!" Miranda exclaimed. "Who's the baby's father? If you're going to have Starlight's baby, it'll be too big for you. Come, I'll put you in Starlight's stall and put a heat lamp in there."

Miranda ran to Higgins' house. A dog barked when she knocked on the door. Miranda heard Higgins shush him.

"Sea Foam's about to foal!" Miranda exclaimed when Higgins opened the door. Colton's dog jumped up on her, begging attention. "Down, Lucky!"

"Yes, I've been watching her. She'll foal anytime this week for sure."

"Why didn't you tell me?" Miranda asked. "We'll have to watch her and get the vet when she starts labor. She's awfully small to have a baby, and with her bad hip, she may need help!"

"I know. I've been checking on her every few hours," Higgins said calmly. "You've been very busy, Miranda, and I haven't seen you all that much."

A surge of sympathy for her old friend washed over Miranda. She knew how much he loved company.

She used to stop in and play a game of checkers with him every once in a while, but hadn't for a long time. She only called on him when she needed him. Yet she truly loved him. She promised herself she'd do better. This was no time to take friendship for granted.

"May I use your phone?" she asked.

"Sure, come on in."

"Margot, I'm glad you answered. Did you know Sea Foam is about to have a baby?"

"Yes. Higgins is helping me watch her."

"Why didn't you tell me?"

"We haven't talked much lately. Besides, I figured you'd notice."

"Well, I want to stay late tonight to watch her."

"Has she started labor?"

"No, not yet. I put her in Starlight's stall with a heat lamp."

"I heard Starlight's gone. I'm sorry," Margot said.

"Thanks. I'll call you if anything happens with Sea Foam, or at the first sign of labor," Miranda promised. "Can I talk to Mom or Dad?"

When they agreed to let her stay until they finished milking, she ran back out to check on Sea Foam.

"How about a game of checkers while we wait?" Miranda suggested when she came back to the bunkhouse.

"Sure, as soon as we have a little supper," Higgins said, putting a bowl of stew and some toast on the table. "Have a chair."

He sat across from her with his own bowl of stew.

The coziness of the little room with a fire crackling in the potbellied stove nearby and the warm food and pleasant companionship melted away the tension that had been building for weeks in Miranda.

"Are you mad at Mr. Taylor for selling his best horses against your advice?"

"No."

"I would be if I were you."

"Not if you were me, because I'm not," Higgins said with a grin, "I know what you mean, but Miranda, Cash has been my friend for a long, long time. If I got mad every time he said or did something I didn't agree with, we would have parted company a long time ago. You have to take people as they are and, even if you can't understand why they do the things they do."

"I don't think I can. When you trust someone and they turn on you, it hurts too bad!"

"Not if you love yourself enough for everyone. If you think your own value depends on what other people think and do, then it can kill you. But if you truly know and love yourself, you can separate what they do. You can sympathize with them and their problems when you know you are not it."

"Not it?"

"Not the problem."

"But don't you just about die of loneliness when your friends desert you?"

"I don't. I am my own best friend. So, when I think a friend's having a problem, I can wait until he asks for my help or stay out of his way while he works it out for himself."

"Kids at school blame me for getting them in trouble. I didn't and I hate being accused of something I didn't do!"

"Yet you believe yourself to be innocent?"

"I am! I didn't tell on anyone, like they think. I never would."

"Then why do you let what they think get you down? Don't let their ideas determine who you are and what you believe."

"I never thought of it that way. But no matter how much I like myself, there's one thing I can't stand, and that's to lose Starlight," Miranda said, unable to hold back tears.

"Like I said, I've known Cash a long time. I've seen him in some very low places, and I've seen him do some desperate things, but he doesn't go back on his word. I don't know why he took Starlight with him, if he did. Maybe someone wanted stud services. But his promises are good, Miranda."

When Sea Foam had not begun labor by nine o'clock. Miranda called home again.

"Please let me stay," she begged. "Higgins has a warm sleeping bag I can use, and I'll sleep in the stall with her. The heat lamp is on so it won't get too cold."

Her parents agreed. Lucky came with her and she felt snug and safe with the little border collie mix curled up against her.

"You miss Colton, don't you?" Miranda asked,

stroking his long, tangled hair. "I do too. Maybe he'll come back and get you, but I wish he'd come back to stay. If I could tell him what Higgins told me tonight, maybe he would."

As Miranda slept, she dreamed of Starlight so vividly that when she heard an equine squeal, she thought it was he.

"Starlight?" she murmured.

One more tortured scream jolted her awake. She wiggled out of the sleeping bag and crawled to Sea Foam, who was lying on her side, straining.

"Hang on, girl, I'll get help."

She ran to the tack shed and called Doctor Talbot. He said he'd be right out. Then she called home. Margot answered.

"She's in labor!" Miranda said.

"I'll wake Dad and be right over," Margot said.

Running to the bunkhouse, Miranda nearly tripped over Lucky who spun excited circles in front of her. Higgins came to the door in his coat and hat.

It was not an easy delivery for Sea Foam; her foal was big and feisty. Doctor Talbot did all he could to assist. Pulling on the front legs he was finally able to bring the head and shoulders through the narrow birth canal. The rest slipped through quickly and as soon as the membranes were cleared from his nose, the hefty colt neighed lustily and scrambled to his feet, fell on his nose, and stumbled up again. Swaying on wobbly legs, he blinked at the audience of people who surrounded him. His mother raised her head, pushed up with her front feet and stood over him.

"Look at him!" Miranda said. "What a cutie."

"He has a star, just like Starlight. Is he going to be black?" Margot asked.

"Possibly," said Higgins who was looking at the mousy gray foal carefully. "Some foals that are born this color turn black when their baby hair sheds. I don't see any white except that star in his forehead."

"What will you name him, girls?" Dad asked. "I guess he belongs to both of you if Starlight is the sire. I don't see how it could be anyone else."

"How about Sea Star, Miranda?" Margot asked.

"I like that," Miranda agreed.

"It's only four hours until bus time, girls. We'd better get you home to bed."

"But Dad, I need to stay and watch Sea Foam and Sea Star in case there's trouble," Miranda argued.

"Is that right, Doc?" Dad asked, as he watched the veterinarian coax Sea Foam to her feet.

"I don't think there's a thing to worry about," Dr. Talbot said as Sea Foam nuzzled her baby and he found her teat. "See, he's already nursing. I've never seen a healthier foal."

Miranda repeated to herself everything she had heard Higgins say about friendship as she boarded the bus the next day. She determined not to take anything anyone said or did that day as a personal attack. *If I know I don't deserve it, I won't let it affect me!*

When she got off the bus, she noticed a lone figure sitting on a swing on the playground. Laurie!

"You look like you just lost your best friend," Miranda said, wryly.

"I did," Laurie said, wiping away a tear, "and I miss her terribly."

"Laurie, I didn't tell . . ."

"I know. I shouldn't have believed Rose Marie when she said you did. You're not like that. Please be my friend again."

"Oh, Laurie. I've missed you so much. It's been awful. It seemed like the bottom fell out of my life when everyone turned against me. When I needed your friendship the most, you treated me worse than everyone else did. At least it hurt more coming from you. I never thought you would do that to me!" Miranda said reproachfully as a sob threatened to choke off her words. She thought again of Higgins advice. Swallowing hard and wiping her eyes, she added. "I'd like to be friends, but I'm scared of being hurt again."

"I can't blame you for not trusting me, but I promise I won't ever be so mean again." Laurie's eyes sparkled with tears.

Miranda hesitated and Laurie continued, "I might not have believed her if you hadn't said you hoped she got caught. That hurt my feelings."

"I've been sorry I said that ever since the words came out of my mouth! But I didn't say it to anyone else, I swear."

"I know that now." Laurie's eyes filled with tears.

"I wish you would've talked to me. Maybe I could've helped you see the real me."

"We can talk now," Laurie said. "If you'll give me another chance, we can tell each other everything like we used to. Now that Rose Marie is gone, I see things more clearly. I miss her though and I hope she's all right."

"Rose Marie is gone? Where?"

"I don't know. She got mad at Mom and Dad and left."

Chapter Sixteen

"Rose Marie is missing?" Miranda asked, incredulous. "Oh Laurie, I'm so sorry!"

"That's why she wasn't in school yesterday. I thought she was locked in her room when I left for school, but Mom tried to get her to answer and she wouldn't. Finally, when Dad got home he took the hinges off the door and the room was empty. There was a note on her bed. It said, *You'll be so glad to find I'm gone you won't mind the money I took.* All the money was gone out of Mom's purse and Dad's jar of change, so we thought she would go back to San Diego, but her mom hasn't heard from her, and there's no record that she ever bought a plane or bus ticket. Dad called the Sheriff and Highway Patrol offices this morning. He's trying to get a search party together, but no one wants to help," Laurie said bitterly.

"But this community always helps when anyone has an emergency," Miranda said.

"Maybe when it's their own. We still don't fit in, Miranda, and most people think Rose Marie was just a trouble maker."

"What's the sheriff doing about it?"

"Nothing. They say it's too soon. Dad's trying to get the newspapers and the TV networks to put her picture on the news, but no luck so far."

"Why did she run away?"

"She got real mad when Dad grounded her for a month. He told her she wasn't going anywhere until she got her act together, quit using drugs, and started treating him and Mom with respect."

"They know she uses drugs?"

"Mom found some in her room," Laurie said. "Rose Marie didn't deny anything; just screamed at Mom for snooping. She called her some horrible names. Mom wasn't meaning to snoop. She was just putting laundry away. Dad came home in the middle of her tirade and tried to interrupt. He said no one talks to his wife like that, but Rose Marie just turned on him. Dad finally took her by the arms and shook her to get her to stop screaming and swearing."

The bell rang and the girls walked slowly to the school as Laurie continued.

"She quit talking then. I never saw her look like that. Her eyes were huge, like she was terrified. Dad apologized for shaking her, but he really didn't do it hard, just enough to get her attention. He said he felt horrible. He has never laid a hand on any of us before. He tried to reason with her, but she wouldn't listen, so he told her she was grounded."

"I haven't been to Shady Hills for over a week," Laurie said at lunch time, "Let's go today and ride."

Tears filled Miranda's eyes as she told Laurie that Mr. Taylor had taken Starlight.

"I'm sure he's going to sell him," she lamented, "Higgins doesn't think he would do such a thing, but why else would he take him?"

"But how could he sell him?" Laurie asked. "He's half yours! Wouldn't you have to sign the papers?"

"I'm just a kid. Mr. Taylor probably knows how to get around that."

"So I don't suppose you want to go to Shady Hills?" Laurie asked.

"I do, to check on Sea Foam and her new baby," Miranda said. "She foaled early this morning."

"Oh, I want to see! Then maybe we can ride. Hey Chris," Laurie said as he walked by with his empty tray, "can Miranda ride Queen after school?"

When Miranda's eyes met Christopher's for just a moment before he looked away, her heart seemed to skip a beat. The empty feeling in the pit of her stomach surprised her.

"I guess so, if she'll clean her stall," Chris said to Laurie.

"I'm right here, Chris!" Miranda said angrily. "You don't have to tell Laurie what to tell me."

"Well?" he asked. "Are you going to clean the stall, or should I ask Higgins?"

"I'll do it whether I ride her or not," Miranda retorted. "I think it's mean to ask Higgins to do your work for you!"

"What's happened between you and Chris?" Laurie asked when Chris followed Jody out of the lunchroom.

"I don't know. He seems to hate me, just like everyone else. Oh well, let him be a jerk," she added quickly, as a tear stung her eye. "See if I care!"

Miranda's heart ached for Starlight and she didn't think she could have borne it without Laurie's renewed friendship. Her classmates gradually came to accept her again when they saw that Laurie had. Maybe it was because Rose Marie was no longer there stirring up sentiment against her.

"I'm sorry to hear you lost your horse," Lisa said to her at lunch one day.

"Thanks," Miranda muttered.

"I always thought Mr. Taylor was mean and cold-hearted, but this is the worst!" Stephanie added.

"Yeah, just when I trusted him," Miranda said. Feeling suddenly disloyal, she added. "Higgins doesn't think he'll actually sell Starlight. Maybe he'll bring him back. Still, he should have asked me!"

"Miranda, did you tell Mr. Alderman that Rose Marie had drugs?" asked Tammy. "Lots of people said you did, but now Laurie says you didn't. I got in a lot of trouble when my parents found out that there was marijuana at the party, so I want to know the truth."

"I didn't tell on anyone," Miranda said, flatly. "But, think what you want."

"I believe you," Lisa said. "Kimberly asked Mr. Alderman, and he said the reason for the raid was because the janitor smelled pot and found ashes in the supply closet. They figured it was one of the new kids, but they wanted to scare everyone."

"Promise not to tell anyone," Stephanie whispered. "I know who was smoking pot in the janitor's closet and it wasn't any of the new kids. It was one of the seniors that's lived here his whole life!"

"Who?" Laurie asked.

"How do you know?" Miranda asked.

"I can't tell. I promised, but believe me, I know!" Stephanie said.

"I still don't know why everyone thought I told," Miranda said.

"When I was really mad at you for things you said about Rose Marie," Laurie said, "I'm afraid I said things to make people think so. I didn't realize how fast the rumor would spread. I'm so sorry, but Rose Marie had me convinced for awhile."

"Chris didn't seem to think it was such a bad thing." Lisa added, "He said, 'what if she did? Maybe she did it so Rose Marie would get help.'"

"Chris ought to know I wouldn't rat on someone. I don't say things about people that I wouldn't say to their faces, but I didn't even do that. I was mad at

Rose Marie so I just ignored her," Miranda said.

"Hey girls, what's the big discussion about?" Dennis asked, placing his tray on the table beside Miranda's.

"If you know a friend is breaking the law, should you tell on them?" Stephanie asked Dennis.

"Oh, yes; the big moral dilemma!" Dennis said. "A teacher asked our social studies class that very question one time. I told her I think ratting on friends is disloyal, no matter what they did."

"I think loyalty is sometimes an excuse for not getting involved," Miranda said.

"So you think people should tell?" Dennis asked her in surprise. "So you did tell Alderman that Rose Marie and I are dopers!"

"I didn't say that, and I didn't tell anyone!" Miranda said hotly. "I'm just saying maybe there isn't a pat answer that works for every situation."

Dennis walked her to their next class, continuing the discussion. Chris and Jody looked up from where they sat at a table, heads together over an open book.

"What are you two looking at?" Dennis asked.

"Some research." Jody answered, blushing.

"What's it to you?" Chris said at the same time.

"Not a thing," Dennis replied, laughing.

Miranda was surprised to see Chris cleaning Queen's stall when she arrived at Shady Hills that afternoon. She was on her way to talk to him when she spotted the Shady Hills pickup and horse van. Mr. Taylor was back! Holding her breath, she ran to Starlight's stall. She slumped to the floor in disappointment when she found it empty. She hadn't realized how much she had hoped that Higgins was right; that Mr. Taylor would bring Starlight home. Taking a deep breath she got up, wiped away her tears, and marched toward the house.

There was no answer when she knocked on the door. She walked toward the garage to see if he'd gone somewhere in his car.

"Miranda, come look!" she heard Elliot shout.

"Shadow had her foal!"

Miranda ran to the box stall where Mr. Taylor gazed at his prize mare.

"It's a colt!" Mr. Taylor said with pride. "Just look at him, Miranda. Black as tar with not a spot of white. I'm going to have him tested. If he's homozygous for the true jet black we're famous for, he'll be the one to take Knight's place. We can even name him Cadillac's Last Knight the Second."

"Is that why you sold Starlight?" Miranda asked, her voice low and barely controlled. "You got rid of the fastest race horse you've ever seen or probably ever will see, just because he has a recessive color gene! And you did it without asking me, which you promised you'd never do!"

"What on earth are you talking about?" Mr. Taylor's jubilance faded quickly.

"You sold Starlight, and you had no right!" she shouted, choking on sobs in spite of her effort to keep back the tears.

"I did no such thing! I know Starlight's half yours. Will be all yours someday. That's why I have such hopes for this lad. Coming out of Shadow by Starlight, he's bound to be a winner!" Mr. Taylor paused and stared at her for a moment. "What do you mean I sold Starlight? Where is he?"

"You're asking me? How would I know? If you brought him back, where did you put him?"

"I didn't take him with me, Miranda. I told you which horses I was taking."

Mr. Taylor looked as if he were in pain. He started to say something more, but turned and walked toward the house, more bent than she'd ever seen him.

Miranda fought the urge to run after him. Was he lying to her? It hurt to see the change that had come over him. One moment he was high on hope over the birth of a beautiful foal, and the next, after Miranda's tirade, he seemed crushed; all joy gone.

As Miranda hesitated, Elliot ran to Mr. Taylor's side. Mr. Taylor rested his hand on Elliot's shoulder. Miranda watched them until they disappeared into the house. Looking back at Shadow and her colt, a picture of all that was good in the world, brought a fresh flood of tears to Miranda's eyes, and sobs choked her. She climbed into the loft, curled up on a pile of dusty hay, and wept as she tried to sort out the feelings that overwhelmed her.

She didn't know how long she'd been there when she heard steps on the ladder.

"Miranda, are you up here?" Chris shouted.

Miranda could see his head and shoulders as he stood on the ladder looking around. She held her breath and didn't move. When he backed down the ladder, disappearing from her view, she let out her breath in a ragged sob.

The sun was low in the western sky when Miranda finally emerged from the barn. She stopped to pet Shadow's foal. He could become the replacement stud for Shady Hills someday. He'd have Starlight's amazing speed, and he had seventy-five percent chance of being homozygous black.

"You might take Knight's place, you little beauty, but you can never take Starlight's place!" Miranda said bursting into tears again.

She was surprised to see Mr. Taylor leaning on the door to Starlight's stall. Elliot stood with his arm around the old man's waist.

"Do you have any idea where Starlight is?" Mr. Taylor asked as Miranda approached. "Have you looked for him?"

"Not in the far pastures. I thought you had him with you!"

"Why would you think that? I had a trailer full of horses to sell. I didn't have room to take one along for the ride."

"But where is he then? He disappeared the day you left!"

"That's over a week ago. We'd better start looking." Mr. Taylor started to the tack shed. "Have your Dad get the jeep."

"Mr. Taylor, I'm sorry I accused you," Miranda said, as they rode in the back seat of the jeep together, "but he was gone the morning after you left, so I just thought . . ."

"Don't fret about it. Maybe someday you'll quit thinking of me as the bad guy. Just hope we find him!"

"What do you think could have happened?"

"Well, maybe he just escaped from his paddock and liked his freedom, but a lot of people wanted that horse. And I owed a lot of them money. Maybe . . ."

"Mr. Taylor, are you all right?"

His face was drawn and gray, and he clutched at his chest. He shook his head in answer to Miranda's question.

"Dad stop!" Miranda yelled. "Mr. Taylor . . ."

Dad slammed on the brakes, bouncing everyone forward. Higgins sitting in the front seat, Elliot, climbing over Miranda to get to his grandfather, and Mr. Taylor all lurched forward, as Dad brought the jeep to a stop.

"Get me out of here," Mr. Taylor moaned, pulling himself up.

They all scrambled out of the jeep and helped Mr. Taylor lie down on a tarp that Higgins pulled from under the seat and spread on the ground. Mr. Taylor curled up on his side, moaning.

"Stay with him," Higgins said. "I'll go for help."

He turned the jeep around and drove away.

"Barry, got pencil and paper?" Mr. Taylor asked in a hoarse whisper. "My will . . . in wall safe . . . write down . . . combination . . ."

Chapter Seventeen

When Mr. Taylor lost consciousness, Dad checked for a pulse. Finding none, he began CPR.

"Grandfather, Grandfather," Elliot screamed, throwing his little body atop the old man's.

Miranda pulled him back and hugged him close as he screamed hysterically, fighting to go to his grand-father. Dad continued the CPR. It was quite dark when Miranda heard sirens. She watched two sets of head-lights dart erratically as the ambulance followed the jeep over the rough terrain. It seemed to take forever. When they stopped, three paramedics jumped out and took over for Dad, rolling Mr. Taylor onto a stretcher and putting him in the ambulance without breaking the rhythm of the chest compressions and mouth to mouth breathing. Miranda and Elliot slipped in, making them-selves as small as possible in a corner.

"Stand back," shouted one of the men, and the other two stood away from Mr. Taylor as flat paddles, attached to a machine with cords were held against Mr. Taylor's chest.

"Now!" someone shouted.

Mr. Taylor's body lurched as electricity lifted it momentarily from the table.

"Again!"

Miranda shuddered, trying to hide Elliot's face, but he pulled free and stared.

"Shhhh," she whispered. "They're doing all they can. Just let them work, and pray."

Mr. Taylor coughed and opened his eyes.

"He's back!" the man with the paddles exclaimed jubilantly. "Let's get him to the hospital."

"How did you kids sneak in here? You have to get out," said one of the attendants.

"No," Miranda said. "Mr. Taylor is the only family Elliot has. "He's not leaving. We won't get in the way, I promise."

Elliot was calm now, though his face was ashen.

"Elliot," Mr. Taylor whispered.

"Don't try to talk, Mr. Taylor," the attendant said, holding an oxygen mask over Mr. Taylor's face.

Pushing it away, Mr. Taylor held out his hand and Elliot squeezed in close and held it.

"Okay, young man, just sit right there and hold his hand," one of the paramedics said.

"I love you, son," Mr. Taylor said, pulling the mask aside as the ambulance turned into the hospital emergency entrance.

The men moved Elliot aside as they opened the back doors and began unloading the stretcher. Gripping Elliot's hand, Miranda followed as Mr. Taylor was wheeled into the emergency room. They were shut out of the cubicle where doctors labored over Mr. Taylor for what seemed like hours. Dad and Higgins joined them as they waited.

"I'll never see him again," Elliot whispered.

"Of course you will. They're taking care of him. He's going to be all right!" Miranda exclaimed.

Elliot shook his head sadly.

"No. I knew when he said he loves me. He never said that before. I wanted him to, but he . . . " Elliot's voice broke, but he bravely continued. "He said them now, because he knew it was his last chance."

When a doctor finally came out of the room and walked toward them, Miranda knew that Elliot was right.

Neither Miranda nor Elliot, who now lived with Miranda's family, were asked to go to school on the days preceding the funeral. Elliot hardly spoke or moved, but lay on the small bed in the sewing room most of the time, refusing to play or eat. Two days after Mr. Taylor's death, Dad called Elliot to come into the living room. Miranda led him by the hand.

"Your Grandfather gave me a combination. He said he had a will in a wall safe. His lawyer has one, dated three years ago, but I hate to go forward with any arrangements or anything else until I find out what his last wishes were," Dad said gently. "I've looked through his house for a safe and can't find one. I know this is hard to think about, but do you know where a safe is?"

Elliot shook his head.

"He never told me. I think he was writing his will the day he died, after Shadow had her colt. I went to the house with him, but he told me to go play while he took care of some business. When I came back, he was folding some papers and putting them in an envelope, but I didn't see where he put them." Elliot explained in the longest speech he had uttered since his grandfather's death.

"Well, I'm going back to look some more," Dad said with a sigh. "Do you want to come with me?"

Elliot hesitated, and Miranda thought he looked paler and more frightened than ever, but he slowly nodded his head and took Miranda's hand.

Inside the Shady Hills Ranch house, Dad went through all the rooms, pulling pictures off the wall to look behind them.

"I searched his office thoroughly, thinking I'd find a wall safe, but there was nothing," Dad said.

"Dad, I'm taking Elliot outside," Miranda said. "This is too hard for him."

Elliot's wide eyes seemed to dominate his thin pale face. They glazed over with a blank expression as his feet dragged. Miranda feared he was about to faint.

"Take a deep breath, Elliot," she said when they stepped into the fresh air. "Slowly, now. Breathe in, breathe out."

When his eyes registered comprehension, they filled with tears. But, he did as Miranda instructed, and color gradually returned to his face.

"You want to go check on the horses?" Miranda asked.

Elliot nodded. As they walked past Starlight's empty stall, Miranda's eyes filled with tears. Sunny nickered to them, and Elliot stopped and petted her. They looked in on the yearlings before turning toward the old barn where Shadow and her colt loafed in the sun. As they climbed over the corral fence, Shadow went into the barn and her foal followed.

"Didn't it look like she was limping? We'd better check," Miranda said.

Shadow was favoring her left front foot, though Miranda could see no wound.

"Her feet need some attention. Looks like her shoe is loose." Miranda said. "Here, Shadow, let me look."

But Shadow sidestepped and ran out of the barn when Miranda approached. Looking for a halter, Miranda opened a door into a room she'd never been in before. It had mahogany paneling on the walls, a large desk in one corner, and a couple of halters and a bridle hung on pegs along one wall. Miranda reached for one of the halters.

"Look behind that calendar," Elliot said, staring at the wall. "I forgot about this room, but Grandfather liked to come here to work on stuff. He said he could

think better close to horses and away from people."

Miranda looked at a calendar in an ornate iron frame. But when she tried to take it from the wall, it wouldn't budge. She found that it was hinged on one side and latched on the other with a small, barely visible hook. When she released the hook, it swung open, revealing the front of a safe with a combination lock.

Miranda clutched a sealed envelope to her chest as she rode home in silence. Elliot did the same thing, his eyes tightly closed. Dad had handed each of them the envelopes when he had opened the safe in which he found dozens of registration papers, deeds, titles, the will, and other documents. On top of everything, had been four legal size envelopes labeled in Mr. Taylor's shaky handwriting. One was to Higgins, one to Dad, and one each to Elliot and Miranda. Dad had opened and read his immediately and then delivered Higgins'. Miranda wanted to be alone when she read hers.

Dear Miranda,

I'll never forget the day you came galloping into my life, riding my horse at breakneck speed without even a bridle or halter. I never told you I admired the daring courage you exhibited then and many times since. You're impulsive nature causes trouble, but your candor and your passion have made a big difference in my life. I've asked your father to take Elliot into your home. I know you will always be a true friend to my grandson. Now that I'm gone, Starlight is all yours to do with as you will. I know you both love to run, so maybe, when you're old enough to ride, you'll put him back in the racing circuit. That's

198

up to you. I am also leaving you three
more of my horses, Ebon's Dark Shadow
and two foals; the yearling filly and her
new colt. Name him what you want.
With love, Cash Taylor

Miranda's stomach, chest, and throat all seemed to seize up in pain. She curled up in a tight ball, burrowing her face into the bed, as hot tears flowed; yet no sound escaped her. When at last she released the block of air past the lump in her throat, it came out in a long, keening cry that she didn't recognize as her own. And then she sobbed, crying convulsively, painfully, and as silently as possible, for she wanted no one to see her agony.

Mr. Taylor loved her, and she realized how very much she loved him and would miss him. And Starlight, now finally hers, a wish she had held in her heart since the day she first laid eyes on him, was gone. She was sure she would never see him again.

"I, Cassius Taylor, being of sound mind, do on this 15th day of March, appoint Barrett Randolph Stevens as guardian of my grandson, Elliot Montgomery, in the event of my death. I appoint Barrett Stevens as executor of my estate and trustee for my grandson's assets until he is of legal age. Barrett Stevens has authority to sell whatever assets must be sold to clear any debts I leave behind. The rest shall ... "

Miranda listened to the reading of Mr. Taylor's will in his attorney's office where she sat with Dad, Higgins, and Elliot around an enormous table. The dark wood was so highly polished that Miranda could see her reflection and everyone else's. She studied the somber expressions on the images in the tabletop. When she looked at her own reflection, she hardly recognized the pinched pale face and large, darkly circled eyes.

Elliot was heir to most of what was left of Mr. Taylor's estate after the debts were paid. Higgins was listed as beneficiary on a life insurance policy and a few items that had sentimental value to him. True to his promise, Mr. Taylor willed Shadow, her foals, and some tack to Miranda. Dad was given the ranch pickup and the big horse van, *"so you can take Miranda to the races when she's ready to race Starlight and her other horses."*

Burying her face in her arms, Miranda cried fresh tears, wondering from what endless fountain they flowed. She couldn't stop crying if she tried. The tears continued when she shut herself into her room at home. She wanted to sleep to escape the pain of reality, hoping to wake up to find that this was all a cruel nightmare.

"Miranda," the voice floated into her dream becoming louder and more insistent.

"Miranda, wake up, honey," the voice persisted, pulling Miranda from the filmy darkness of her dreams. "You've got to get ready for the funeral. We need to leave in forty minutes, and you need a shower."

Opening her eyes, Miranda looked into Mom's worried face. Funeral. Miranda closed her eyes again and felt them sting until tears slipped from beneath her closed lids. She didn't want to go to the funeral. She didn't want to see anyone or anyone to see her. Life seemed to have lost its point.

"Miranda, I know you're hurting. You've locked yourself away and done nothing but sleep for the past two days," Mom said. "It's time to think of someone else. Do you think it's going to be easy for Elliot today? He's been asking for you, Miranda. Get up now and get in the shower."

Mom's tone of voice moved Miranda to action, because it left no room for argument. Slipping out from under the covers, she walked, a bit unsteadily, to the bathroom. The warm water washing over her felt good, bringing life back into her body, which had been mostly numb since Mr. Taylor's death.

Astonished at how drawn and pale Elliot appeared in his gray suit and sweater, Miranda regretted that she had abandoned him in his sorrow. He held out his hand to her as they headed for the car.

"I'm sorry you're feeling so sad, Miranda," Elliot whispered. "I understand."

"Oh, Elliot, thanks, but you . . . I'm sure you feel worse than I do. I've been selfish. I . . . "

"It's okay, Miranda."

Gray clouds filled the sky, and a cold gust of wind

assailed the group of people huddled around the cas-ket that was poised over the grave. Miranda held Elliot's hand tightly, and looked at the faces of the few people braving the weather to pay their last respects. Laurie, who seemed to be thinner than Miranda had ever seen her, stood with her mother and father. When she looked up and saw Miranda staring, she raised her gloved hand to her mouth and blew Miranda a kiss.

Chris stood between his parents, staring at the coffin. Miranda noticed with surprise that he was taller than his mother. He had shot up when she wasn't pay-ing attention. No wonder Jody was so crazy about him. Chris was actually good looking! He looked at her just as this thought crossed her mind. His smile was kind and his blue eyes filled with sympathy.

Higgins sat in a chair next to the minister at the head of the grave. He stood, and with his thin voice filled with emotion, he told stories about his early days with Cash Taylor.

"Cash had a determination I always admired, even when I called it hardheaded stubbornness. But it was that stubborn independence that built his empire. And it was his honesty and loyalty that won him so many friends. Cash was the best friend I ever had." Higgins' voice broke and he sat down.

A movement behind Higgins caught Miranda's eye. Someone was walking, almost running across the lawn to join the group just as the minister began to pray. It was Colton.

Chapter Eighteen

"Miranda, I want you to come with me to Shady Hills this morning," Dad said the next day. "It's time you checked on your horses."

Miranda wanted to protest that her horse was gone. But she knew Dad was talking about Shadow and her little Knight. She forced herself to obey. She dutifully fed and watered Shadow. She watched to see if she was still limping, but whatever had lodged in her hoof must have come out, for she trotted around the corral without a sign of pain. The colt was frisky and full of life. Watching him brought a smile to her lips until she thought of Starlight. Was this baby supposed to take his place? No. She turned away, tears in her eyes. No horse, human, or anything would ever make her forget Starlight.

A car rattled across the cattle guard, catching her

attention. There was something very familiar in the sound, and she left the corral to investigate.

Colton was stepping out of his car when she rounded the corner of the stable row.

"Miranda, it's great to see you," he shouted.

"You, too, Colton. Where have you been? I wish you'd come back sooner."

"Me too," Colton said bitterly. "How was I to know the old man would die before . . . I didn't want him to go without resolving our differences. You were right. I took his temper too personally. He gave me my first chance, and I wish I had thanked him."

His voice caught and he looked away, blinking his eyes. Miranda changed the subject.

"What have you been doing?"

"I'm riding for a big ranch in Kentucky. It pays pretty good and I like it. They have some very high-powered thoroughbreds. None like Starlight, though. I don't think there'll ever be another horse like him. I'd like to see him before I go."

"You can't. He's not here," Miranda said, looking at the ground.

"Where is he?"

"I'd give anything to know. We can't find him! I've looked everywhere on this ranch. He's been gone two weeks now."

"You think someone stole him?"

"There's no other explanation. I would have started searching sooner, but I thought Mr. Taylor had taken him. When I found out he hadn't, Mr. Taylor had his heart attack and . . . ," Miranda's voice broke.

"I'm so sorry!" Colton exclaimed. "Maybe I can help. There are places on the web that you can post pictures of lost or stolen horses. Has anyone reported it to the authorities?"

"I think Dad has," Miranda said sadly. "I don't think there's any hope of them finding him. They don't even care enough to look for a lost person, so I don't think they'd try to find a horse."

"You know a lost person?"

"Rose Marie," Miranda said.

"What? Oh no!" Colton's face paled. After swallowing hard he continued, "I was hoping to see her while I was here."

"Forget her, Colton. I hope they find her and I hope she's okay, but she isn't the girl for you. You can do better."

"What makes you think you know what's good for me?"

"I just meant you're a good, honest person, and she's, well, so different. The way she treated you was rotten and you deserve better."

"Let me be the judge of that. How long has she been gone and what are they doing to find her?" Colton demanded.

"She's been gone over two weeks, and I think everyone but the Langleys have forgotten her." Miranda was sorry she didn't have better news for Colton whose face was dark with grief or anger.

"I'm going to arrange a sale," Dad announced at the supper table that evening. "Mr. Taylor has so much debt, I think we'll have to sell most of his assets, including Shady Hills. I've already got a couple of cattle ranchers from out of state looking at it."

News of another auction depressed Miranda even more. Shady Hills was like a second home to her.

"What about the horses Mr. Taylor gave me, and Sea Foam and Sunny and Queen and Lady?"

"We'll bring them here. If Chris and Laurie want to board theirs here, there is plenty of room."

"But we'll have to make new corrals and stables won't we?"

"I'm sure we can make do, Miranda."

"Miranda," Dad called when she arrived at Shady Hills after school. "The attorney just delivered all the papers on the horses. I have the registration transfer papers for Shadow and her filly, Knight's Ebony Shadow. They need your signature and then I'll mail them to the Registry."

Miranda took the pen dad handed her and signed where he indicated.

"Congratulations, Mandy. You have yourself three new horses," Dad said. "Here's the form for Shadow's colt. Have you thought of a name for him?"

Tears filled Miranda's eyes. She shook her head, and hurried toward the old barn, crossing the corral where Shadow stood with her foal. Confused by the sudden rush of grief and anger, she wanted to be alone.

Climbing the ladder to the hay loft, she tried to understand her feelings. Shadow was one of the prettiest horses in the world. She had wanted Mr. Taylor to buy her long before he decided to do it. Yet, even though people seemed to think her colt would take Starlight's place, he was a reminder that she had lost the best friend she would ever have. She couldn't possibly love the foal as long as Starlight was missing. She fell into the hay and sobbed.

When she gradually became aware of a presence beside her, she looked up to see Elliot. His face was wet with tears, though he made no sound. She reached for his hand, and he gripped hers tightly. Each aware of the other's sorrow and respectful of each other's need to cry without talking, they sat together for a long time.

"Did you hear, Miranda?" Stephanie said as Miranda walked past her and Tammy in the hallway the next morning. "Bergmans' store was broken into last night."

"Was anyone hurt?"

"No. Mr. Bergman didn't know until this morning. He called my dad when he couldn't get hold of the sheriff."

"There's Chris," Tammy said. "Chris, is it true about your store?" she yelled.

"Yeah, the front window was broken and glass scattered everywhere. Dad put plywood over the window for now," Chris answered.

"What did they take?" Miranda asked.

"Not much. Maybe some groceries."

"Who do you think did it?" asked Stephanie.

"Don't know," Chris said. "Well, gotta get to class."

When Miranda put her tray on the table next to Laurie at lunchtime, Chris surprised her by setting his tray next to hers.

"Mind if I sit here?" he asked.

"No," Miranda said, "you're free to sit wherever you want."

"There's something I wanted to tell you about the break in," Chris said in a low voice.

"What?"

"It's something I noticed when I came out of the store," he said. "You know, we haven't had any big snow storms for awhile and the ground is pretty dry. But there's a low spot where there's a little mud. I saw a horse hoof print there. When I was walking to school I saw fresh horse manure on the other side of the road."

"So you think whoever robbed your store was riding a horse?" Miranda asked.

"That's what I think."

"That's weird! A lot of people around here ride horses, but none of them would break into your store for food."

Chris shrugged and sighed.

"That's why I didn't tell anyone else, but I thought you might . . . "

"Hey you two," Dennis boomed from behind Miranda, "What's the big discussion about?"

"None of your business," Chris growled. "Sorry I mentioned it, Miranda."

Chris got up and left before Miranda could say anything. She looked up at Dennis when he put his hand on her shoulder.

"I just got my driver's license and my parents are letting me take the car into Bozeman to see a movie Friday night. Want to go with me? It's all I want from you for my birthday."

"You're fifteen?" Miranda asked.

"Yeah. That's what's great about Montana. Where I came from I couldn't have had a license until I turned sixteen, and then it's very restricted."

"I still have another year to wait. I'll turn fourteen . . . " Miranda stopped, surprised. Her birthday was coming up soon and she'd forgotten all about it.

"Well, you going to the movie with me?"

"No, my parents won't let me date until I'm at least fifteen."

"So don't tell them it's a date. They let you go to Tammy's party with me."

"I'm sure they won't again. Besides, I have other things to do."

"Like what?" Dennis challenged.

"Like nothing that concerns you!" Miranda snapped, suddenly angry that Dennis seemed to doubt her word.

"Fine!" Dennis shouted. "I'll find someone who appreciates the offer! Hey, Jody, wait up."

Miranda slid into her desk just as the bell rang

after lunch. She was suddenly very weary. It was going to be a long afternoon! She could hardly wait for Spring Break the last week of March. Maybe Laurie could come spend the days of freedom with her, helping prepare for the sale. *I hope I don't see a single boy but Elliot,* Miranda thought. *They are impossible to understand!* On her way to the next class, she told Laurie of her plans.

"Oh, Miranda," Laurie said. "I won't be here. We're going to California."

"Why? You never told me."

"Mom just decided late last night after talking to Aunt Jillian for two hours! They're both so upset about Rose Marie that they don't know whether to kill or comfort each other."

"Oh," Miranda said. "It doesn't sound like a very fun vacation."

"I know. It'll be more like a funeral," Laurie said, blinking back a tear. "Mom said she'll go without us, if Dad and I don't want to come, but Dad says this is a time for the family to stick together."

The next week was busy, but Miranda felt empty as she helped prepare for the sale that was to take place Thursday and Friday. Her time was divided between looking after Kort and Kaden and helping Dad, Mom, Grandma, and Grandpa box up items from Mr. Taylor's house, tack shed, and barns. Small items were put on wagons and tables in the indoor arena, in case of snow or rain. They gathered horses from pastures and stuck numbers on their hips.

Miranda had just helped Dad run the yearlings into a large paddock near the barn when the Bergmans' pickup pulled up beside them. Miranda was surprised to see Christopher get out of the driver's side.

"Hi Chris," Dad said. "Help us put the horses that aren't for sale back into the small pasture behind the barn, if you have time."

"Sure," Chris said, vaulting the fence. "Then may I take Miranda for a drive?"

"Be extremely careful, and have her home before dark," Dad said.

Miranda stared at her father in amazement. Didn't he know that Chris didn't have a license to drive? But Dad was already rushing to the next task. Miranda's surprise turned to anger that neither Chris nor Dad had asked her if she wanted to go. She didn't protest, however, for she felt she couldn't stand to be at Shady Hills another minute. Even with all the work to be done, without Starlight and Mr. Taylor, the place was gloomy.

"Where are we going?" Miranda asked. "Did your parents actually give you permission to take the truck?"

Chris didn't answer as he eased the pickup onto the county road. He handled it like a pro, for like most of the kids in the area, he had been driving on back roads since he was nine or ten. He was taking driver's education and so had a learner's permit and would get his license when he turned fifteen in the summer.

"Chris!" Miranda demanded. "Why did you come get me? If this is some kind of mean trick, let me out right now."

"Just trust me a minute, will you?" Chris growled, as he turned the pickup into a narrow mountain road.

In a few miles, they came to a big snowdrift that blocked the muddy, rutted road.

"We walk from here," Chris said. "I brought snowshoes."

"I'm not going anywhere until you tell me what's going on and why we're here!" Miranda shouted at Chris who was in the truck bed, throwing a pair of snow shoes in her direction.

"Look at the ground, Miranda," Chris said. "We're going to follow those tracks."

Miranda looked down at the imprint of horse-shoes that headed up the hill, through the snow.

Chapter Nineteen

Miranda scrutinized the tracks. The horse was shod on all but one foot. They were a few days old and covered by snowmobile tracks in places.

"Why? There are tracks going both ways. Whoever rode up here has come back out. People around here ride into the mountains all the time, so what makes you so interested in these tracks?

"Bill and his dad went snowmobiling this morning. According to Bill there are a lot more tracks higher up. Fresh ones too. Why are there fresh tracks up above but none down here? Sounds like whoever rode that horse, didn't come out yet. I think if we find the rider, we'll find a thief!"

"You could have told me sooner," Miranda said. "Hurry. Put on your snowshoes and let's go!"

"I would have brought the snowmobile, but Dad

had it locked in the garage," Chris said.

"So you don't have permission. I didn't think so!" Miranda exclaimed.

"Mom and Dad are on a business trip and won't be back until late tonight. I didn't have any way to ask them," Chris said.

"Why did you choose me to go with you?" Miranda asked as they trudged up the hill. "I thought you hated me."

"I don't hate you, and I thought you'd want to be in on this."

"Why?"

"Just because. If you don't, you can go back. I didn't think you'd be afraid . . ."

"Afraid! You know very well I'm not, Christopher Bergman!" Miranda shouted. "I just don't like being treated like dirt for months on end and then have you acting like you own me. You could have explained it to me and then asked if I wanted to come."

"Sorry if I treated you like dirt. I didn't think I did," Chris said.

"You know very well you did. So did everyone in the school. You thought I told on Rose Marie for having drugs at Tammy's party. I never . . ."

"I never thought you told on anyone. Not for long, anyway. I know you better than that."

"You acted just like everyone else, only worse. The only time you'd speak to me was when you had something mean to say."

"Not true! I tried several times . . . I'm really sorry,

Miranda," Chris said, stopping to look at her. "I was a jerk. But it wasn't because I thought you were ratting on Rose Marie or anyone else. It was because . . .," Chris rolled his eyes and started walking again.

"It was because what?" Miranda demanded. "I want to know."

"I didn't like . . . never mind. It doesn't matter. "

"It matters to me!" Miranda said, stopping. "Look at me, Chris. I think I have a right to know what I did to make you mad."

"You got all google-eyed over the new kid in school, just like the rest of the girls. A city slicker with his weird clothes and fancy hairdo walks in, and all the girls want to go out with him."

"Google-eyed! That's ridiculous and totally unfair. I never did any such thing."

"Yeah, right. You're the one who went to the party with him!"

"So? That didn't mean anything. I only went with him because he asked me first. Besides, you were so busy looking at Jody, you didn't even want to talk to me or go with me to Shady Hills or anything like we used to do. Talk about google-eyed! I think you should look in the mirror."

"I wouldn't have asked her to the party if you would've gone with me."

"Well, I guess you should be glad that I said no, then," Miranda exclaimed, passing Chris as she stomped up the hill, "because you sure are crazy about her now!"

"Am not!" Chris shouted, following her. "You

don't know a thing about how I feel."

"Well if you don't like her you shouldn't be cuddling up to her in public. The way you two act at school, I'd hate to see what you do in private!"

"Yeah? Well, I bet it's nothing compared to what you and Dennis do!"

"You don't know anything about me and Dennis!" Miranda shouted back. "I wish you'd quit assuming you know everything about my personal life, because you don't have a clue!"

Powered by anger, Miranda strode up the hill at a good clip. Her breath came in ragged puffs and her legs burned from want of oxygen. Still she pushed on, unwilling to show weakness to Chris who, she could hear, was right behind her.

"Miranda, stop!" Chris finally shouted.

Miranda stopped, and suddenly felt dizzy and sick to her stomach. She bent over and braced her hands on her knees as she drew in great gulps of air.

"What?" she said when she could finally talk.

"I thought I was going to pass out if I kept trying to keep up with you," Chris said laughing. "I wasn't about to let you show me up, though."

Miranda laughed weakly. "I'm glad you stopped me. I think I'd have collapsed before I admitted I was getting tired, because I didn't think you were."

"Miranda," Chris said so softly that Miranda had to turn to face him to hear what he was saying.

"Miranda," Chris began again. "I'm sorry I, well, sorry I acted so mad at you. I was just crazy jealous.

There now I've said it and you can hate me if you want to, but it's the truth. I couldn't stand seeing you and Dennis together, and he was right there every time I looked at you. And if I ever got a chance to talk to you alone, he'd come out of nowhere and interrupt!"

"You were jealous of Dennis?" Miranda asked, smiling. "I didn't know you cared about me enough to be jealous."

"Duh, Miranda. How could you not know? I've had a crush on you ever since the first day you came to school at the end of fourth grade!" Chris's face turned redder than it already was from the exertion of hiking.

"I didn't know. You were always so mean to me. You picked on me more than anyone else."

"I know. I guess that's what guys do when they like a girl they don't think they have a chance with. I knew I was fat and freckled and you're so pretty, I didn't think you'd notice me, so I teased to get your attention."

"You were kind of fat and awfully freckled," Miranda admitted, staring at him. "But you aren't anymore. Jeez, you've gotten tall and you're not really fat at all anymore. And I like your freckles."

"What about Dennis?"

"What about him?"

"Are you in love with him?"

"Are you crazy? Of course not!"

"What do you mean, 'of course not,' like it's an impossible idea? Even I have to admit he's good looking and he obviously likes you — a lot!"

"What about Jody? It's obvious to everyone in

school that you two are in love."

"We are not!"

"Then why are you always chasing after her? I guess I shouldn't say chasing, because she obviously isn't running!"

"She never liked me, and I never liked her for anything more than a friend. She has a huge crush on Dennis and wanted to make him jealous. I thought if you saw me with another girl you'd get to thinking that I wasn't such a loser after all, and maybe even get a little jealous!"

"Chris! That's pathetic!" Miranda exclaimed. "I mean it's sad. How could you think you needed some other girl to show me you're not a loser! I've known that ever since fifth grade!"

"Really? Were you a little jealous then?"

"I don't think so. I was terribly hurt that you didn't want to be my friend anymore. You deserted me when I needed you the most. And that made me mad!"

"So you weren't going out with Dennis to make me jealous?"

"Good grief, no! I wasn't 'going out' with him at all. I never liked him any more than any of the other boys in school. He was just there, always talking to me. I was just trying not to be rude!"

There was an awkward silence as the two stared at each other.

"Miranda," Chris finally said. "Will you forgive me? Can we be friends again?"

"Sure, Chris," Miranda said, swallowing hard as

her heart, which had finally slowed down to normal after the strenuous climb, began beating hard and fast again.

She felt weak in the knees, and her stomach did some kind of flip-flop, as if she were on some scary carnival ride when Chris stepped up next to her and leaned close. He whispered, "More than friends, maybe?"

Miranda's mouth went dry and a lump in her throat prevented her from answering. As he leaned closer, she closed her eyes, waiting.

"Ooops!" Chris yelled, his body falling against her, pushing her sideways into the snow.

"I'm so sorry," he said as he struggled to get up without pushing her deeper into the snow. "I shouldn't have tried that with these snowshoes on. I love you."

At least that's what Miranda thought he said. The last three words were spoken so quickly and quietly that Miranda wondered if she had only imagined them. It couldn't be wishful thinking, could it? *No*, she told herself. *He probably said he didn't mean to shove me.* Embarrassed and relieved that the awkward moment had passed, she laughed so hard she could hardly get up. Chris offered her a hand, as he laughed too.

"I guess we'd better keep going if we're going to find those horse tracks," she said, clumsily maneuvering the cumbersome snow shoes.

Doubts flooded her as she remembered how much Chris had hurt her. How could she have forgiven him so quickly, she wondered. Unsure of what had passed between them, she tried to gather her thoughts.

"What I don't get," she said as she trudged up the trail, "is why you turned on me just when I needed a friend the most."

"I'm sorry. I realize now how awful that time was for you," Chris said. "I wasn't thinking right."

"It went on for so long, I thought you hated me," she said, not willing to let it drop so easily.

"I didn't mean for it to last that long, believe me," Chris said. "I kept trying to talk to you, but there was Dennis, every time! He'd take over like he owned you. I thought I didn't have a chance compared to him, and I thought you were happy with him."

"I didn't encourage him. I'd get mad, too, when he interrupted, but you didn't need to walk away when I was trying to talk to you."

"I'm sorry I gave up so easy, but I was confused. I didn't want you thinking of me as, well, just an old friend instead of — well, uh, someone you could get to really like — for, uh, more than that, uh, someday, maybe," stammered Chris, suddenly surging ahead as the trail narrowed, giving Miranda no chance to reply.

The trail leveled out as it passed through a grove of leafless aspen trees. As Miranda rounded a corner, she saw a side road leading from the main trail. She stopped and examined the tracks. Fresh snowmobile tracks went both ways, but she couldn't see which way the horse tracks went.

"The wind has blown them," Chris said, examining the ground closely. "When we get back into a more sheltered spot, we should be able to pick them up again."

"Yeah, but which way?"

"Well, I guess I could go one way and you the other, just until one of us sees something," Chris suggested.

Miranda took the trail to the left, and Chris continued straight ahead.

"See anything yet?" Chris yelled.

"There's something, but I can't tell if it's horse tracks or something else. How about you?"

"Nothing this way but snowmobile tracks, and the wind hasn't blown here in the trees. I'm coming your way. Wait up."

"Look, isn't that a cabin up there in the trees?" Miranda asked when Chris came up beside her.

"Yeah. I think you're right."

In a few more yards, Miranda picked up some clearly visible horse tracks. They no longer followed the snowmobile tracks, but led toward the cabin. She increased the pace, moving as fast as she could on the awkward webbed feet strapped to her boots. Chris stepped up beside her as the trail widened.

"I wonder if the thief is holed up in that cabin. There are more tracks around here and they're fresh. I don't see any smoke coming out of the chimney, though," Chris observed.

"Look! Is that a horse? Oh, it is! A black horse!" Miranda squealed with excitement. "Could it be . . . ?"

A shrill whinny cut through the air and the horse charged toward them. Miranda tried to run and fell face first into the snow. She sat up and tore at the buckles on the snowshoes. Kicking them off, she got to her feet just as the horse skidded to a stop and thrust his nose into her face.

"Starlight! Oh, my Starlight," she cried as she scrambled to her feet and threw her arms around his neck. She shed tears of joy and relief.

"Listen!" Chris shouted. "Did you hear that?"

"What?"

"Listen!" he repeated. "Isn't that someone calling for help?"

Miranda lifted her head and held her breath. She heard it too. A faint cry from the direction of the cabin, calling, "Help! Please, please, help me."

Chapter Twenty

A search of the cabin revealed a pile of clothes on a chair, a sleeping bag on the cot that stood in the corner, and some canned goods on the rough boards that formed shelves near the crude wood stove.

"Where are you?" Chris shouted.

"Help! Here, behind the cabin!"

There was a small back door and both Miranda and Chris rushed to it, crowding through together.

"Over here! Please hurry," the weak voice was broken by a sob.

A crumpled form lay on the snow-covered ground in the edge of a grove of firs near the corner of the cabin. A mass of snarled black hair, flecked with pine needles and wood chips, lifted as Miranda stared. Puffy red eyes met hers in a miserable plea.

"Rose Marie?" Miranda asked in amazement.

"Rose Marie! What happened to you? What are you doing here?"

"My leg hurts and I'm freezing. Please help!"

"You're bleeding!" Chris shouted, dropping to his knees beside Miranda at Rose Marie's side.

The snow was stained pink and scuffed with finger marks, as if Rose Marie had been digging with her bare hands.

"Look!" Chris yelled as he dug deeper into the snow. A huge steel trap with sharp jagged teeth cut into Rose Marie's leg just above the ankle. Chris pressed the release. Rose Marie screamed.

"Sorry, sorry!" Chris exclaimed jerking back. "I was just trying to take it off."

"I tried to dig it out, but it cuts in deeper every time I move," Rose Marie said. "It's fastened to something under the snow. Oh, I'm so cold!"

"A blanket! I'll be right back!" Miranda said.

When she came back with a woolen blanket, a sleeping bag and a pillow, Chris was digging with a shovel.

"Ow!" Rose Marie cried. "Don't pull on it!"

"Sorry," Chris apologized again. "I thought I was far enough away I wouldn't hit the chain."

He tossed the shovel aside and began digging with his gloved hands. Miranda tucked the sleeping bag and pillow underneath Rose Marie as well as she could and tucked the blanket in around her.

"We've got to get you off that wet snow," Miranda said. "Your clothes are soaked. We must get you dry."

She ran back inside to find a change of clothes and a towel. A pair of jeans and a sweat shirt hung on the back of a chair. Unable to find a towel, she picked up a T-shirt from the floor. Rose Marie was so exhausted that she kept falling asleep as Miranda tried to help her get out of the wet shirt and into the dry one. By the time she finished, Rose Marie lay still, either unconscious or asleep. There was no way to change the wet jeans. Chris found the end of the chain and unfastened it from a log that was buried deep in the snow.

"Is she breathing?" he asked.

"Yes," Miranda said, placing her head on Rose Marie's chest, "and her heart's beating but awfully slow!"

"We've got to get some help before it's too late!" Chris said. "Maybe I can get this trap off her leg while she's sleeping."

Rose Marie moaned when Chris pried on the trap. Blood began oozing from the wound as the teeth began to pull out.

"I can't spring it," Chris said. "Maybe if we both try."

"Wait. Leave it on," Miranda said. Let's see if we can drag her into the cabin and get a fire going."

"With this thing on her leg?"

"It might be keeping her from bleeding. If one of those teeth is in a big blood vessel and we pull it out, we might not be able to stop the bleeding before we get her to a hospital."

"How can we move her with the trap on her leg?" Chris asked. "And the cabin isn't any warmer than it is out here. Maybe you should ride Starlight for help, and I'll stay with her and try to keep her awake."

"I don't know if she can last that long. By the time I get someone to come up here it might be too late."

"What do you suggest?"

"I don't know. Maybe we can build a fire and get the cabin warm," Miranda decided, getting to her feet. "Stay with her."

Miranda hurried inside and began searching for fire starter. She found a can of matches, but no paper or wood. She looked around the room, which was growing dim as the sun slid behind clouds just above the western ridge of mountains. Hanging high on one wall was a large toboggan. Standing on a chair, she could just reach it. Heavier than she expected, it unbalanced her, and she fell to the floor, toboggan on top of her.

"What happened?" Chris shouted from the doorway. "Miranda, are you all right?"

"Ouch!" Miranda said. "Just a little bruised, I think. Help me get this outside."

"What's your idea?" Chris asked as they slid the toboggan up next to Rose Marie.

"Get the mattress off the cot and put it on the toboggan. Then we'll roll her onto it and tie her on. We'll wrap her in every blanket there is and figure out a way to secure the trap so it doesn't cut into her. Starlight will pull her down the mountain."

She looked up at her horse, affection for him

flooding over her. He hadn't moved far from them and stood watching her. She couldn't understand how he came to be here with Rose Marie. Why would she steal her horse? She hadn't even wanted to ride since she came here. That girl had a lot of explaining to do, if they could get her back to civilization alive.

After some ineffectual tries, they finally managed to prop Rose Marie's leg, trap and all, on a pillow, tying the trap to the toboggan so it couldn't slide off. They covered it as well as they could with one blanket, wrapping the rest tightly around Rose Marie's body and lashing it all down with a rope. It was fairly dark by the time they finished, but the moon was rising, and they could make out the trail. Miranda found his saddle and bridle in a lean-to behind the cabin.

"Get on behind me and hold the rope. I don't dare tie it to the saddle horn," Miranda said.

"No!" Chris shouted, as he strapped on his snowshoes. "It's too steep. The toboggan would run into Starlight. I'll walk it down."

Starlight plunged through the snow, sometimes sinking to his belly. Chris, with a tight hold on the toboggan trudged behind. There was no sound from Rose Marie as the toboggan glided noiselessly over the snow.

When the hill wasn't too steep, and the trail clear of trees, Chris took off his snowshoes, stood, his feet on either side of Rose Marie, and rode the gliding toboggan past Miranda and Starlight. Starlight lunged through the snow in an effort to keep up.

Before long, a glare of light illuminated the road.

A little farther around the curve, Miranda saw long shadows on the snow and the silhouettes of two people next to Chris's truck.

"Drat! I don't have the key, and Chris locked the truck," said the unmistakable voice of Mr. Bergman. "I'll have to drive home and get the spare."

"Dad!" Chris yelled. "Wait! We're coming!"

"Miranda? Are you there? Are you okay?"

"Dad! We need an ambulance. Quick!"

"What? For who? Is that Starlight?"

Miranda didn't answer until she pulled up in front of her father and dove into his outstretched arms.

"I'm so glad you're here! It's Rose Marie. She'll die if she doesn't get to a hospital soon," Miranda cried.

Chris handed the keys to his father, and Mr. Bergman got on his mobile phone. Chris bent over Rose Marie's still form.

"She's still breathing!" he said again. "She even moaned a little. Rose Marie, wake up. The ambulance will be here soon."

It wasn't soon, however, for they were many miles from the nearest medical center. They debated about trying to put Rose Marie in one of the cars but were afraid to move her with the trap still attached to her leg. Dad agreed that it might be risky to take it off.

"Let's lift the toboggan into the back of your mini van," Dad suggested. "It'll get her out of the wind, even if we have to leave the back hatch open."

"Sure. We'll have to take the back seats out, but that won't take long."

"How did you find us?" Miranda asked as the men moved the seats.

"I was worried when Chris didn't have you back before dark, so I called the Bergmans," Dad explained. "They had just gotten home and found Chris's note. I met him and we drove together in Bergmans' van."

"You left a note, Chris?"

"Thank God he did!" Mr. Bergman exclaimed. "It said he had to borrow the truck and was going as far as he could up North Meadow Creek. Said it was an emergency, which I didn't believe until now."

"How did you know it was an emergency?" Miranda asked Chris.

"I didn't. I thought we were going to find a thief and come back and tell the cops where he was. But, in case there was any trouble, I thought it would be good if people knew where we were."

When Dad and Mr. Bergman lifted Rose Marie into the van, she moaned softly, then cried out, and began to sob.

"Good, I can close the back door with the toboggan inside. I'll let the paramedics know I'm taking her to the hospital myself," Mr. Bergman said. "Chris, come with me to keep an eye on her. Barry, take my pickup."

"It's a long ride to Shady Hills," Miranda said to her dad. "I'd better get started."

"I know a rancher down the road a mile. He'll let us leave Starlight at his place until I can get back with a horse trailer," Dad said.

Chapter Twenty-one

Propped up on white pillows Rose Marie looked drawn and pale, her dark brown eyes and black hair in deep contrast to the white sheets of the hospital bed. She managed a weak smile as Miranda and Christopher walked in the next morning. There was an IV dripping fluid into a vein in the back of Rose Marie's thin hand. Her leg was elevated and swathed in thick bandages with only her bruised toes sticking out.

"Miranda, I'm very sorry I took your horse," Rose Marie whispered.

"Why did you?" Miranda asked. When Rose Marie closed her eyes, she added. "You don't have to tell me if it hurts to talk,"

"You and Chris saved my life! And Starlight!" Rose Marie said. "How did you happen to find me? I was sure I was going to die all alone out there."

Her eyes filled with tears and her voice failed her. Miranda squeezed her arm and whispered.

"It was Chris. Maybe he should be a detective," Miranda said.

"I'll never be able to repay you," Rose Marie said to Chris, grasping his hand.

"Ah, you don't owe me anything," Chris said. "I wasn't really expecting to find you. But I had a hunch someone was hiding out with a horse. If I hadn't thought

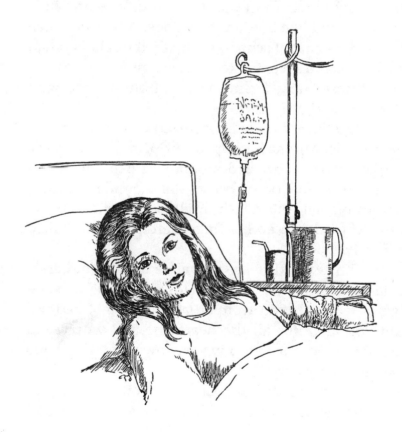

it might be Starlight, and I wanted to do something special for Miranda, I probably wouldn't have come."

"I owe you an explanation," Rose Marie said to Miranda. "I should say confession. I don't expect you to forgive me, but I've got to tell you."

"You can tell me later if you want," Miranda said, alarmed at Rose Marie's weak, raspy voice.

"No. I want to get it over with," Rose Marie whispered. "I was furious at you. Laurie was always talking about how brave, funny, and fun you were and how much I would like you. I was jealous. And then when they had the raid at school, I actually thought you had told on me and I wanted to get revenge."

"Rose Marie!" came a shout from the doorway. "Are you all right?"

A petite red-haired, blue-eyed woman rushed to the bedside. Miranda stepped out of the way. Laurie and her parents crowded around the bed, and Chris moved to the foot of the bed to stand beside Miranda, slipping his hand into hers in an almost automatic movement. Miranda closed her fingers around his and held on firmly.

"I'm so glad to see you alive that I could cry!" exclaimed the redhead, though Miranda couldn't see a sign of tears. "If you weren't laid up in that bed, I'd skin you alive for all the heartache and worry you caused me. Do you have any idea how many gray hairs you put on my head?"

Miranda didn't see any. The woman, who was obviously Sheree Langley's sister, looked as if she had just stepped out of a fashion magazine. Rose Marie frowned.

"I'm sorry, Mom."

"We're just thankful you're safe!" Mrs. Langley said. "Are you hurt much? How's your leg?"

"I'm sorry I worried you and Uncle Preston," Rose Marie said as tears filled her eyes. "It was stupid, but it gave me time to think. I promise nothing like this will ever happen again. Can you possibly forgive me?"

"Of course we can," Mr. Langley said. "Like your aunt said, we're just glad you're okay. Now what about your leg?"

"The doctor says I'll have some pretty bad scars and might want to get plastic surgery some day. And there's infection. If they can't stop it from spreading, they might have to amputate. But if the antibiotics do their job, I should heal without a limp or anything."

"Are you hurt anywhere else?" asked Laurie's mom, squeezing Rose Marie's hand.

"The doctor's worried about pneumonia, but the antibiotics should help that too. I was so cold that I didn't think I'd ever get warm again. He said I had hypothermia and probably wouldn't have lived much longer." Tears brightened her eyes again.

Laurie crowded past her parents to kiss her cousin.

"How'd you get here so soon?" Miranda asked Laurie.

"The sheriff had our number at Aunt Jillian's house. He called us as soon as he got the 911 call from

Mr. Bergman. We got the first plane out of San Diego."

Miranda rose early on Thursday morning, did her chores, and helped her mother prepare food for the potluck. They set off early to Shady Hills for the auction. Lou Seifert, the rancher from Oregon who had bought Shady Hills, met them as they walked to the indoor arena. He planned to turn Shady Hills into a cattle operation and asked Dad to work for him long enough to change some of the fences and turn the shed row of stables into a loafing shed. He'd be moving his herd of red Angus as soon as the sale was over.

"I may keep a few horses and let my wife give riding lessons," he said. "You might steer us in the right direction when it comes to that part of the sale. I'd like to buy at least two or three to go with the pair I'll be bringing with me from Oregon."

"Higgins can probably help you with that better than I can," Dad said. "He knows every horse on the ranch; its history, bloodlines, temperament, and training. I'm going to load up the horses that aren't for sale and take them home before the auction starts."

Miranda ran to help him, and Chris arrived as she was loading Shadow and her foal.

"I'll get Queen," Chris said. "You want to help me catch Shooting Star?"

"Miranda, look at Sea Foam," Margot interrupted as she led her little mare to the trailer.

Miranda turned to see Margot and Elliot approaching, leading Sea Foam with Sea Star prancing ahead of them.

Miranda petted the foal and looked at Sea Foam. "What about her?" she asked.

"Don't you see? Watch." Margot said, as she urged the little mare to circle around her in a trot.

"She isn't limping!" Miranda exclaimed. "Lead her away from me, Mar, so I can watch from behind."

The little mare walked briskly, without a sign of a limp. She had a spring in her step and brightness in her eyes that made Miranda wonder how much pain the displaced hip had caused.

"Wow, I can't believe it. There's Doc Talbot. Let's ask him how this happened!" Miranda exclaimed.

"Just be happy about it," Margot said.

"No, what if it's just a fluke? I want to know if she'll be all right from now on."

"Why wouldn't she be?"

"I don't know, but the people we bought her from said it was a deformity she was born with, and nothing could be done for it. They also said it didn't hurt her. Now I think it did."

When Miranda returned from talking to the Doctor Talbot, Margot had her horse loaded and was helping Elliot bring his. They stopped to listen to Miranda.

"Doc Talbot doesn't think it was a genetic defect, but more likely an accident or injury at birth. And he doesn't think it was her hip. He thinks her pelvis was out of place or something. He said a combination of things could have healed her. The hormones the body produced when she was pregnant probably relaxed the ligaments or muscles enough that when she had the foal, the pelvis got straightened out or something like that. He said that pulling the large colt was kind of like putting her in traction, and it worked."

"Will it ever go back to the way it was?"

"Nope, he thinks she'll be fine from now on."

"Was she in pain before?"

"Yeah. The vet thinks so, and now that I see the difference in her, I'm pretty sure she was," Miranda said, and added when she saw tears flood Margot's eyes, "but look on the bright side. She feels great now, and we gave her as good a life as she could have had anywhere."

The Langleys arrived a little before the sale was scheduled to begin at ten. Miranda, just getting back from taking the horses home, ran to help them carry hot dishes to the garage where a potluck was being arranged. Passing Mr. Taylor's Cadillac forsaken in a row of other vehicles and machinery awaiting the sale, Miranda blinked back tears before turning to Laurie.

"How's Rose Marie?" she asked.

"She's great. Colton's at the hospital with her."

"Colton?" Miranda asked in surprise. "I thought he left for Kentucky."

"He did, but he came back. When he heard we found Rose Marie, he told his boss he had to leave on a family emergency and flew back."

Miranda frowned. "Family emergency? I never thought Colton would tell a lie."

"I don't think he considered it a lie. I think he'd

like to make Rose Marie more than just a friend."

"Well, I hope she doesn't break his heart again. I told him . . .," Miranda stopped realizing that what she started to say would hurt her friend's feelings.

"Rose Marie wants you to come. She really wants to talk to you. She should get out of the hospital Saturday. Will you come that day?"

Relaxing on the couch in the Langley's cozy sitting room, Miranda faced the warm glow of the fireplace, lit against the chill of a spring snowstorm. Chris sat next to her, and Rose Marie, sitting on the edge of an easy chair faced them. Colton stood behind her, hands on her shoulders.

"I have to tell you my story, Miranda. You might hate me, but you will anyway, and, well, I just have to let you know I'm different now. I learned a lot in those two long weeks in the mountains.

"I got so mad at Uncle Preston when he grounded me, I decided to run away. I was going to steal his car, but I couldn't find the keys. I tried to hitchhike, but the first person to stop was a rancher. He asked all kinds of questions about where I was going. I was afraid he'd tell Uncle Preston if I said I was trying to get to the interstate, so I said the first thing I could think of. I told him I was going to Shady Hills to go riding. He said he was going right by there and would take me all the way to the house.

"When he let me out, I walked to the stables, pretending I had a plan. Starlight was sticking his head out of the door and nickered at me. I petted him and he acted like he liked me. He made me remember what it was I loved about horses when I was little. I felt a connection. Besides, I, umm, well I was still really mad at you for telling on me. I know you didn't, but I thought you did, so a crazy idea popped into my head. If I took Starlight, I could get away and get even with you at the same time. I'm so sorry, Miranda."

"You got even, that's for sure," Miranda said. "I don't think there's any way you could have hurt me more, but how did you end up in the mountains?"

"I kept riding, trying to figure out what I was going to do with Starlight when I got far enough away that I could hitchhike. I thought there was a way over the mountain, and I figured Butte had to be over there someplace. I hoped I could sell Starlight for enough money to get a plane ticket.

"I didn't know exactly where the trails were but I'd heard Laurie talk about going up to the top and seeing trails going down the other side when you all went camping up there. I thought if I just followed the trail, I'd find it. I almost turned around when I ran into snow. But at first it wasn't deep, and Starlight just kept going like it was nothing."

"I'm surprised Starlight didn't give you any trouble," Miranda said, feeling betrayed by her horse.

"I was too, and he did some, at first, but he seemed pretty excited about going somewhere. I always got along with the horses I rode. I think they know I like them, and I do know how to ride. I took lessons for three years.

"Anyway, pretty soon I got scared. I didn't know what to do," Rose Marie continued. "The snow was getting deep and heavy, and it was getting dark. I thought of turning around, but I thought I might be closer to the other side. After the sun went down, I got cold.

"I talked to Starlight a lot, or else I would've gone crazy. He seemed to be listening and he kept going. It seemed like we'd been going forever, and we were still going up hill. I didn't know how much farther to the top, or how far to any town on the other side. When the moon came up, I saw the cabin. It had everything I needed to spend the night. There was wood piled by the stove, paper, matches, lots of canned food and dry cereal and stuff on the shelf, sleeping bags, blankets, even a bucket of water by the sink. Of course it had ice on it, but I put it on the stove after I got the fire going. I also had food with me that I took from home.

"I had a lot of time to think, Miranda. After four days, I ran out of cigarettes and pot. I wanted some, but they weren't worth going back for."

"What did you do with Starlight? What did you feed him?"

"I just tied him to a tree so he wouldn't run off. The next morning, I found some hay and grain in the lean-to on the side of the cabin. I melted snow on the stove for him to drink.

"I kept trying to decide if I should go back or try to go on, but even though I was lonely, and wanted something to smoke, I got to feeling like, well, it's hard

to explain. I liked being able to take care of myself —
building fires, cooking, feeding Starlight. I felt... I don't
know, proud I guess. It's a feeling I never had before.

"I finally stopped tying Starlight to a tree. It just
didn't seem right. He stayed close to the cabin and came
when I called. I rode a lot during the day. It snowed
often and covered up all our tracks coming in, so whenever I'd hear snowmobiles, I'd stay out of sight."

Miranda struggled with mixed feelings, as she
listened to Rose Marie. Starlight had betrayed her. She
had imagined that he would buck with any stranger
who tried to take him. *He must have sensed something in
Rose Marie that I missed,* she thought.

"Then I ran out of food," Rose Marie went on. "I
wasn't ready to go back to civilization but I had to eat.
So I rode back to town, broke into Bergmans' store, and
got all the food I could carry. I started to get some cigarettes too, but decided I could get along without them.
They just didn't seem to go with my life as a hermit,"
Rose Marie laughed weakly.

"I ran out of wood several times, but I found
some dead branches back in the trees. There was an axe
in the cabin and I got good at using it. I used up the last
of the wood the night before you two came. I went out
to get more the next morning so I could cook breakfast.
I broke through the snow where you found me. There
was sagebrush or something keeping the snow from
packing in tight around the trap and I stepped right into
it. I would have died...," Rose Marie's voice trailed off
as tears filled her eyes again.

"But what I want to tell you," she continued, "is that I'm not the same person I was before. I was selfish and angry. I valued the wrong things. When Mom went back to California this morning, I could have gone with her, but I would have just gone back to my old life; partying with my old friends. I belong to Montana now. It saved my life even though it almost took it."

Miranda reached for Rose Marie's hand.

"Will you forgive me and let me be your friend?" Rose Marie asked.

"Sure I will!" Miranda said, smiling.

"No peeking now," Dad said as he led Miranda across the yard on her fourteenth birthday. "Step up. Okay, this way. Now open your eyes.

"SURPRISE!"

Miranda's eyes flew open at the roar of dozens of voices. For a moment, she wasn't sure where she was. She stared at a wide aisle, lined with horse stalls on each side. Halters hung from hooks made of horseshoes beside each stall door. Miranda looked at her father in confusion.

"How do you like what I did with the old milk barn, Miranda?"

"I. . . I thought you were making a workshop. It's beautiful!"

Dad had been working in the old dairy barn ever since Grandpa sold his cows. Being absorbed by other problems and projects, Miranda hadn't peeked in since he started. She looked for her friends in the crowd that was now singing a rousing rendition of "Happy Birthday." There was Chris next to Laurie and Rose Marie, leaning on her crutches. Colton stood next to her. Bill was behind Laurie, and all of Miranda's classmates were there. Higgins sat on a hay bale beaming at her with pride. Mom helped Kort carry a cake, ablaze with candles, and Margot bounced Kaden on her hip. Elliot stood nearby.

When the fanfare was over, Miranda walked from stall to stall, looking at Dad's handiwork. The cow stanchions had been replaced by box stalls with two-part doors that opened into the wide walkway. Artistically carved nameplates were attached to each door. Starlight's stall was in the very center on the east side, with Queen's directly across from his. Starlight nickered at her and scraped the inside of the door with his foot, as if telling her to hurry. She stroked his face as tears of joy sprang to her eyes.

In the next stall were Shadow and her colt.

"I've got to give him a name," Miranda said. "I've been thinking about it and decided to call him Starless Knight, since he hasn't a speck of white on him, and I think Mr. Taylor would be honored if we call him Knight."

Colton came to stand beside her. "You're getting quite a spread here, Miranda. Do you think you could use some help with training, and maybe even let me ride for you in some races?"

"I thought you were working in Kentucky."

"I decided to stay in Montana. I have a job at

Bergmans' store, but I could work here in my spare time. You wouldn't have to pay me."

"I've been thinking about racing. I'll be old enough to ride in one more year. I think I'll wait until then to enter Starlight, but we could use some help training Shooting Star. She's old enough to start, and is she ever fast! Right, Chris?"

"Sure. Miranda, do you remember when you and Laurie said you were going to have a horse ranch together, that first day Laurie came to Country View when we were in fifth grade?" Chris asked.

"Yeah! That was the day I socked you in the nose, and you dared me to ride Starlight. It was the day I fell in love with him and vowed he'd be mine someday, but I don't think I really believed it."

"Well," Chris went on, "wouldn't you say your dream has come true?"

"He's right, Miranda!" Laurie exclaimed. "I thought we'd be grown up before that dream came true, if it ever did. Look at all the horses we have here at Greene's dairy. We don't own the land, but all three of us own horses."

"Not Greene's Dairy anymore," Grandpa said. "This is a horse ranch now. You kids need to come up with another name."

"How about the Stevens, Langley, and Bergman Ranch," Chris suggested, "Oh, and Montgomery," he added, looking at Elliot.

"That sounds like a law firm!" Miranda exclaimed. "Of course you have a part in it, Chris, and

Margot and Elliot have horses here, too. Look at all the Stars we have! There's Starlight, Shooting Star, Moonbeam, Sea Star, Star Prince, and Starless Knight. And Elliot told me that when Sunny foals, he's going to name her foal Super Nova, whether it's a colt or a filly. I say we call our horse ranch Heavenly Acres."

Epilogue

Miranda had spent the weekend in Billings at the state music festival, and though it had been fun, and she and Laurie won an award with their duet, it was great to be home. Chris Bergman was at Heavenly Acres to meet her and they walked to the stable together.

"Let's take Starlight and Queen through the river pasture and ride over to see Higgins," Miranda suggested.

Higgins had moved into the Caruthers' house after the sale. He could have lived with his nephew in Bozeman, but he preferred the country. Miranda was glad. She loved having him nearby and consulted him often for advice on the care and training of the horses.

As Chris and Miranda came out of the stable with their horses, Margot and Elliot were hitching Sea Foam to Elliot's two-wheeled cart. Little Sea Star dashed back and forth between his mother and anything else that caught his interest. And he was curious about everything he saw. Miranda laughed when he pranced up to Little Brother who was sauntering toward them. Sea Star skidded to a stop, snorted, and sniffed. When Little Brother licked his nose, he squealed, pivoted, and dashed back to Sea Foam, kicking his heels in the air.

"We're going to see Higgins," Margot said.

"That's where we're headed," Miranda replied. "We'll meet you there."

Elliot clicked at Sea Foam and drove out to the county road. Margot, sitting proudly beside him, looked back at the foal who was trotting behind. Miranda waved, and Margot waved back with a bright smile. As Miranda rode slowly toward the pasture gate she watched Shadow, Lady, and Sunny grazing in what used to be the calf pasture, their foals cavorting nearby. Miranda smiled at the size of her growing horse ranch. The yearlings and weanlings were in the pasture nearest the Caruthers's house where Higgins could keep an eye on them.

Her thoughts turned to the old groom with affection. Though he was getting stooped and gray, he checked on the horses several times a day. He noticed everything about them and could tell Miranda what each one's strengths would be. He was ever aware of the splendor of his natural surroundings, often pointing out a new flower, a rare bird, or the way the sun beams played on the mountains behind the house.

It was a joy to be with him for he always seemed to see the good in every situation and never complained. Either she, Margot, or Elliot; sometimes all three, sometimes with Laurie and Christopher, visited him every day, often staying to play a checkers tournament or just listen to him talk about the old days. Elliot, who loved to hear the stories about his grandfather, often spent the night with Higgins.

"I feel close to Grandfather when I'm with Higgins," he told Miranda one day. "He loved Grandfather, too. He played with him when Grandfather was just my age, and they rode in this same little cart together back in Texas a long time ago."

Today, Christopher and Miranda rode slowly through the tall pasture grass, weaving in and out of willow thickets and aspen groves. When they crossed a small stream, they allowed the horses to drink. Deep contentment filled Miranda's heart as she surveyed the hills and mountains, the feathery clouds, and the lush green meadows. They rode on in silence, Miranda entranced in her own deep thoughts until Starlight stopped at yet another gate. Chris had opened the last two they had come to.

"I'll get this one," Miranda said, dismounting.

It was a four strand, barbed wire gate with two stay posts in the center of it. It fastened simply by slipping the end post into a wire loop near the ground and pulling another wire loop over the top of it. This gate was tight, and Miranda, pulling as hard as she could, couldn't get it closed.

"Let me help," Chris said, dismounting.

He reached his arm around hers. Miranda immediately forgot the gate as a thrill went through her. She turned to face him and he dropped the gate. His

face was so close to hers, it took her breath away. Staring into his blue eyes, she knew he felt the same way.

"Miranda, will you go out with me?" Chris asked blushing, "I mean, be my girlfriend — you know."

Miranda stepped back and picked up the gate as she tried to formulate an answer.

"Here, I'll get that," Chris said, closing the gate with no apparent difficulty.

"I don't think we have to promise anything, Chris," Miranda finally answered. "You've been one of my two very best friends in the world for a long time. That isn't going to change."

"You know what I mean, Miranda," Chris said. "I . . . I mean . . . I, er, do you like me more than, well, you know, more than just a friend?"

"I think so. I mean, sometimes when we are close I feel like there are butterflies in my stomach."

Chris stepped in front of her again — close! He leaned down, for he was a few inches taller than she was now. Miranda stared into his eyes as her heart rate quickened. When his lips brushed hers, she closed her eyes and kissed him back. Her first kiss was like fireworks going off inside her. She reveled in it for a few moments before she pulled away.

"Chris! I wasn't going to kiss anyone until I was at least sixteen. I didn't know I'd feel like this."

"Me either, even though I've been wanting to kiss you for a long time," Chris said. "But we don't have to kiss, if you don't want to. As long as I know you feel like I do, I'm happy. When I thought I didn't have a chance with you, it made me care about you more than ever."

"I really like you, too," she whispered. "I began to realize how much when I thought you didn't like me. But I'm scared that if we say we're, you know, boyfriend and girlfriend, it'll change us. I've seen kids get goofy and possessive and, well, they let their feelings spoil their friendship. Promise me that won't happen to us, because I want you to always be my friend."

Their eyes locked, and the intensity Miranda felt was reflected in Chris's face.

"I promise," he whispered.

For this and other titles in this series
inquire at your favorite book store,
gift shop, saddlery, or feed store,
or purchase them directly from the publisher.
Ordering information on back of this page.

Happy Reading and Riding to You!

Send check or money order to:

Raven Publishing, Inc.

P.O. Box 2866

Norris, MT 59745

$9.00 per book plus $2.00 shipping and handling
for one and $.50 for each additional book.

Or order on line at *www.ravenpublishing.net*

For more information, e-mail:

info@ravenpublishing.net

Phone: *406-685-3545*

Toll Free: 866-685-3545

Fax: *406-685-3599*

Name_____

Address_____

City_____State_____Zip_____

Please send me:

_____copies of **Miranda and Starlight**

_____copies of **Starlight's Courage**

_____copies of **Starlight, Star Bright**

_____copies of **Starlight's Shooting Star**

_____copies of **Starlight Shines for Miranda**

_____copies of **Starlight Comes Home**